What Readers Are Saying about Forbidden Doors

"Nothing I have seen provides better spiritual equipment for today's youth to fight and win the spiritual battle raging around them than Bill Myers's Forbidden Doors series. Every Christian family should have the whole set."

> C. Peter Wagner
> President Global Harvest Ministries

"During the past 18 years as my husband and I have been involved in youth ministry, we have seen a definite need for these books. Bill fills the need with comedy, romance, action, and riveting suspense with clear teaching. It's a nonstop page-turner!"

> Robin Jones Gunn
> Author, Christy Miller series

"Bill Myers's books will help equip families. It's interesting, too, that the Sunday school curriculum market, for which I write, is examining topics such as reincarnation and out-of-body experiences. The Forbidden Doors books are timely."

> Carla Williams
> Mother and freelance author

"Fast-moving, exciting, and loaded with straightforward answers to tough questions, Forbidden Doors is Bill Myers at his best."

> Jon Henderson
> Author

The Curse

James Riordan

Based on the Forbidden Doors series created by Bill Myers

Tyndale House Publishers, Inc.
Wheaton, Illinois

Visit Tyndale's exciting Web site at www.tyndale.com

Published in association with the literary agency of Alive
Communications, Inc., 1465 Kelly Johnson Blvd., Suite 320,
Colorado Springs, CO 80920.

ISBN 0-8423-5966-4

Printed in the United States of America.

02 01 00 99 98 97
7   6   5   4   3   2   1

For my daughter,
Elicia, who gives
me such joy.

Listen to me! You can pray for anything, and if you believe, you will have it.

Mark 11:24

1

There was an ominous clunk under the Boeing 737. Rebecca stiffened and threw a nervous look over to her younger brother, Scott. He was sitting to her left, next to the window.

"It's just the landing gear coming down," he said, doing his best to sound like an experienced air traveler.

Becka nodded. She took a deep breath and tried to release her sweaty grip on the armrests. It didn't work. She didn't like flying. Not at all. Come to think of it, Becka didn't like the whole purpose of this trip.

Who did Z, the mysterious adviser on the Internet, think she was, anyway? What was he doing sending her and her brother off to Louisiana to help some girl caught up in voodoo? Granted, they'd had lots of experience battling the supernatural lately. First there were those kids caught up in the Ouija board, then all that reincarnation stuff, and then those satanists. And let's not forget the so-called ghosts up at that house, the counterfeit angel, and that last encounter with a supposed UFO.

But voodoo in Louisiana? Becka didn't know a thing about voodoo. She barely knew anything about Louisiana.

Fortunately Mom had a cousin who lived in the area, so she'd insisted on coming along with them to visit her. Good ol' Mom. Becka looked to her right, where her mother rested comfortably, her eyes closed. Maybe the trip would do her some good. Ever since Dad died she'd been fretting and working and worrying nonstop. This trip just might give her the rest she needed.

Clunk . . . clunk . . . brang!

Then again . . .

It was the same sound, only louder. Rebecca looked to Scott, hoping for more reassurance. "What's that clunking?" she asked.

Scott shrugged. "I don't know, but it's the 'brang' that bothers me."

So much for reassurance.

Suddenly the intercom came on. "Ladies and gentlemen, this is your pilot. There seems to be a problem with the landing gear. . . ."

The collective gasp from the passengers did little to help Becka relax.

"I've radioed ahead for emergency measures. . . ."

Rebecca felt her mother's hand rest on top of hers. Becka turned to Mom.

"Don't worry," Mom said. "We'll be all right."

Don't worry?! Yeah, right.

The pilot's voice resumed. "The ground crew is going to spray the runway with foam."

"Foam?" Scott exclaimed. "Does he mean like shaving cream?"

"I'll advise you as the situation develops," the pilot continued. "Please try to remain calm."

Clunk-clunk-BRAANG.

The sound was even louder.

Rebecca looked past Scott and out the window. They were flying low over New Orleans and dropping fast. Suddenly the plane banked to the left, and she saw the airport. She wished she hadn't. Several large tanker trucks were spraying down the runway, and there were fire trucks and ambulances everywhere.

Now it was the head flight attendant's turn to be on the mike. "Please make sure your seat belts are fastened low and secured across your lap. Then bend over as far as you can in the seat, keeping your head down. Hold a pillow to your face with one hand, and wrap your other arm around your knees."

Rebecca fought the fear down and threw a look at her mother. The woman had her eyes shut and was praying. Not a bad idea.

CLUNK-CLUNK-BRAANG

Another attendant hurried through the aisle, passing out pillows. She tried to appear calm but failed miserably.

The plane banked back to the right. Rebecca laid her face down on the pillow in her lap and gave her seat belt another tug.

"This is the captain. . . . We are about to land on the foam. . . . Please hold on."

CLUNK-CLUNK-BRAANG

"Don't be alarmed," he said. "That's just

the landing gear mechanism. . . . I'll keep trying it as we come in."

Becka remained hunched over with her face on the pillow. She could feel the plane dropping, and still the landing gear was not coming down. They were going to land with no wheels!

CLUNK-CLUNK-BRAANG
CLUNK-CLUNK-BRAANG

She turned to see Scotty, who was staring back at her from his pillow. He tried to force an encouraging grin, but there was no missing the concern in his face.

She turned to look at Mom. The woman's eyes were still closed, and she was still praying.

CLUNK-CLUNK-BRAANG!
CLUNK-CLUNK-BRAANG!

Becka's thoughts shot to Ryan, her boyfriend back home. If she died, how would he handle the news? And her friends, Julie, Krissi, Philip? Then she thought of Dad. Of perhaps seeing him soon. Too soon. It was this final thought that jolted her back to the present and caused her to join in her mother's prayers. It wasn't that she didn't want to see Dad again; she just had a few more things to do first.

CLUNK-CLUNK-BRAANG!
CLUNK-CLUNK-BRAANG!!
CLUNK-CLUNK-CLUNK DAREEEEEEEE . . .

Something was different!

The plane veered sharply upward. Rebecca couldn't resist the temptation to sit up and glance out the window.

"This is your pilot. The landing gear has engaged. We are out of danger. I repeat. We are out of danger. I'm making another pass to land on a different runway. We'll be safe on the ground in a few moments."

"Thank you, Lord." Mom's prayer was audible now and full of relief as she sat up, then reached over and hugged both of her children. "Thank you . . ."

Becka breathed a sigh of relief. They were safe. At least for now. But all the same, she couldn't help wondering if this was some sort of omen. A warning of the dangers that were about to begin.

~

The three o'clock bell at Sorrento High rang, and throngs of kids poured out of the old, weathered schoolhouse. One girl, about fifteen, slowed her pace as she headed for the bus. No one talked to her, and her clothes were more ragged than most—too shabby to be fashionable and too conservative to be alternative.

Sara Thomas had never fit in. She had never felt like she belonged, no matter where she was. As she approached the school bus and stepped inside, she steeled herself, waiting for the taunts.

None came. Just the usual after-school chatter.

Carefully she took a seat, stealing a glance to the rear of the bus. Ronnie Fitzgerald and John Noey were engrossed in a tattoo magazine.

Maybe they'd forget about her today.

With a swoosh and a thud the door closed, and the bus jerked forward.

Maybe today would be different.

Then again, maybe not. They had traveled less than a mile when it began. . . .

"Hey, Rags, you shopping at Goodwill or the Salvation Army these days?"

Sara recognized Ronnie's shrill, nasal voice.

"Hey! I'm talking to you."

She didn't turn around.

"I heard Goodwill's got a special on those cruddy, stained sweaters you like so much," Noey said snidely.

Before she could catch herself, Sara glanced down at the brown chocolate stain on her yellow sweater.

The boys roared.

"Is that from a candy bar or did your dog do a number on it?" Ronnie shouted.

Most of the others on the bus smirked and snickered. A few laughed right out loud.

Sara stared out the window as the taunts continued. As always, she tried to block out the voices. And, as always, she failed. But not for long.

Soon, she thought to herself. *Soon they'll pay. They'll both pay.*

She reached into her purse and clutched the tiny cloth-and-straw doll. Already she was thinking about her revenge.

And already she was starting to smile.

∾

Aunt Myrna's farmhouse was simple but clean. The furniture inside was made mostly of dark wood. The chairs looked like they'd been there a hundred years . . . and could easily last another hundred.

After Rebecca dropped her bags off in the small attic room that she would be using, she headed down to the kitchen, grabbed an apple out of the fruit basket, and strolled out to the front porch.

It was hot and humid, which reminded her of her childhood days in South America. It had been nearly a year since Dad had been killed and they had had to move from Brazil back to California. But the humidity, the heat, and the smells of the rich vegetation here in Louisiana sent her mind drifting back to the jungles.

Unlike California, everything in Louisiana was lush and wild. Plant life seemed to explode all around. And the water. There was water everywhere. Lakes, ponds, marshes. Most of the land around the bayou was swamp, but even the dry land never really felt dry. Even so, it was beautiful.

Still, Becka was nervous. Very nervous. Z had given them so little information. Just that a young girl named Sara Thomas lived in this area and that she was in serious trouble—caught up in some kind of voodoo. Z had also stressed that Rebecca and Scott were not to be afraid.

"Your training is complete," he had said. "Go in his authority."

"His authority." God's authority. Becka had certainly seen God's work in the past. There was no denying that. But even now as she looked around, she felt a strange sense of—what? Apprehension? Uncertainty?

Those other times she'd always been on her home turf. But this . . . being in a strange place, helping somebody she didn't even know . . . it all made her nervous. Very nervous.

She sat on the front steps eating the apple as she mulled over her thoughts. The late-afternoon sun shimmered on the vast sea of sugarcane that spread out before her. Wind quietly rippled through the cane, making the stalks appear like great scarecrows with arms beckoning her to come closer. Closer. Clos—

Something grabbed her hand.

Rebecca let out a gasp and turned to see a small goat eight inches from her face. It was gobbling down the last of her apple.

"Aunt Myrna!" she shrieked. "There's an animal loose out here!"

"He won't bother you none."

Rebecca turned, startled. It was another voice. And it was calling from the field. She tried to locate the source of the voice while keeping one eye on the goat, just in case he decided to go for a finger or two.

A young man walked out of the field. Becka figured he was about seventeen. Tall and lean, his black features were handsome, in a rugged sort of way.

He nodded to the goat. "That's Lukey. He's more pet than farm animal." He entered the yard and stuffed his hands into his pockets. "Try scratching his nose. He likes that."

"Oh, that's OK," Rebecca said quickly. "I'd rather not just now." Then, rising to her feet, she said, "You must be John Garrett. Aunt Myrna said you'd be coming."

The young man nodded. "Miss Myrna said

I should be showing you and your brother around the place some."

"So let's get started," Scott said, appearing suddenly in the doorway. "Wow. Cool goat. C'mere, boy." He crossed to the animal, and it immediately started rubbing its head against his arm. "Hey!" Scott looked up with a broad smile. "He likes me."

"He likes everybody," John Garrett said, already turning back toward the field. "We better get started if we're going. The foreman's called a meeting of all us hands, and it should be starting pretty soon."

Scott went to walk beside John, and Rebecca fell in behind.

In seconds the two boys were hitting it off. Becka could only marvel. Her brother got along with everybody. In fact, when they'd moved to California, he fit in like he'd always been there. Unfortunately, it wasn't so easy for Becka to make friends. She figured that was partly why she felt so uncomfortable about this trip. She didn't like the idea of barging into a total stranger's life, even if they were supposed to help her.

But that was only part of the reason. There was something else. A feeling. Something eerie . . . something she couldn't quite explain but that she couldn't shake off.

"John," she called, trying to sound casual, "do you know anything about voodoo?"

He glanced back at her and laughed. "Not much. 'Cept my grandpa used to speak Gumbo all the time."

"Gumbo?" she asked.

"It's kind of a mixed-up mesh of African. A lot of the people into voodoo speak it. But you really got to be careful who you talk to about voodoo around these parts."

"Why's that?" Scott asked.

"Lots of folks believe in it, and if you upset them, they'd just as soon drop a curse on you as look at you."

Becka felt a tiny shiver run across her back. "A curse? Does stuff like that really happen?"

"Oh yeah. I heard about this woman who lived down the road from my father. She made an old *mambo* mad, and the *mambo* put a curse on her."

"*Mambo?*" Scott echoed with a snort. "Sounds like some kind of dance step."

John shot him a knowing look. "They're like high priestesses. And they're nothing to mess with."

"So what happened to this woman?" Scott asked.

"A gopher started growing in her belly."

"A what?" Scott exclaimed.

"Oh yeah. Folks said you could even see it moving around in her, and she'd be screaming in pain 'cause it was gnawing at her insides. Finally she died, but I guess it was pretty horrible."

"That's awful!" Rebecca shuddered. "Did you ever see her?"

John shook his head. "No, but my father's cousin said he did. Not only that, I also heard about an old man who refused to pay the *hungan* for helping him get back his wife." At Scott's raised eyebrows John explained. "A *hungan* is like the male version of a *mambo*—the high priest. The man who wouldn't pay carried a powerful root with him at all times so the *hungan* couldn't work no magic on him while he was alive. But when he died and they took him to the morgue, his body started shaking all over the place. And when they cut him open, they found he was full of scorpions!"

"Come on—scorpions?" Scott scoffed.

But Becka was not scoffing. In fact she was growing more uneasy by the moment. "How about him?" she asked. "Did you see him?"

John shook his head again. "No, this happened before I was born. But I believe it."

Scott shook his head, his face filled with skepticism. "I don't know. Sounds pretty fantastic to me. Like something out of a class B horror flick."

"Maybe so," John continued. "But one thing I do know, and that's to never cross Big Sweet. I've seen his magic, and it's powerful."

"Who's Big Sweet?" Scott asked.

"You don't know who Big Sweet is? He's Miss Myrna's foreman. He's head of the harvest crew. Been picking sugarcane all his life. That's why they call him Big Sweet."

"Why's he so dangerous?" Becka asked.

"He's the local *hungan*. People say his father was a disciple of Marie Leveau, you know, the Queen of Conjure. She was a powerful *mambo* who used to live in the French Quarter of New Orleans."

"And you're afraid of him?" Rebecca asked.

"Everybody's afraid of Big Sweet." John turned back to Becka. There was something about his look that caused a cold knot to form deep in her stomach. "Everybody's afraid . . . and you'd better be, too."

Suddenly a horn bellowed across the fields. John spun toward the sound, looking genuinely startled.

"What's that?" Scott asked.

The other boy started moving away from them toward the sound. Becka and Scott exchanged concerned glances. John was clearly very nervous and anxious. "That's Big Sweet's horn," he said. "It's his conch shell. The meeting's starting. I gotta go."

"What about showing us the rest of the farm?" Scotty called as John moved away.

"I can take you into the swamp tomorrow after chores. But I gotta go now."

"Yeah, but—"

"Look, I can't be late. I gotta go." With that he disappeared into the cane.

"John!" Scott called. "Hey, John! Hold on a minute."

But there was no answer.

Scott turned to Becka. She knew her expression held the same concern she saw in her brother's face. The horn continued to bellow. Finally Becka cleared her throat. "I, uh, I guess we'd better head back."

"Yeah. I can't wait to get the lowdown on all this stuff from Z tonight. I'll bet he knows about this Big Sweet guy."

"And Sara Thomas," Becka reminded him.

"Right," Scotty said, "but the more we learn about Big Sweet, the faster we'll be able to blow him away."

"Blow him away?" Rebecca felt herself growing impatient with her brother. "Come on, Scotty. You sound like a Schwarzenegger movie."

"That's me!" Scott threw a few mock karate kicks. "Scott Williams, Demon Terminator."

"Scott, this isn't a joke."

"What's the matter? Afraid Big Sweet may slap a curse on you?"

"Stop it."

"Afraid he might hatch a lizard in your ear or give you a monkey face? Hmmm, looks like somebody's already done that."

"Scotty!"

"Come on, Beck—lighten up." Then, looking across the field, he had an idea. "Let's save ourselves a little time and take a short-cut through the cane."

Becka began to protest, but her brother had already started out. And there was one thing about Scotty—when he made up his mind to do something, there was no stopping him. With a heavy sigh she followed.

The cane was well over their heads, but he was right, by taking this shortcut they'd get back to the house a lot faster. And with all the uneasiness she had been feeling out there, especially now that they were alone . . . well, the sooner they got home, the better.

Unfortunately, "sooner" was way too long now that Scotty was in his teasing mode. Brothers, what a pain. He kept jumping around and darting between the stalks of cane like some ghoul.

"Oggity-boogity. Me Big Sweet. Cast-um big curse on you."

"Knock it off," Becka muttered between clenched teeth. She was going to bean him if he kept it up.

"Big Sweet turn you into little mouse if you not careful."

"Scott, you know you're not supposed to joke around with—"

"Oggity-boogity." He leaped even higher into the air.

"Scotty."

"Oggity-boogity . . . Oggity-boog—OW!"

Suddenly he crumpled to the ground.

Becka's heart pounded as she raced to his side. "What happened? Are you OK?"

"I twisted my ankle," he whined. "Owwww."

Becka knew it served him right, but he was clearly in pain, so now was not the time to bring it up. Instead, she reached out and carefully touched his ankle.

"Ouch!" he yelped. "That hurts!"

"Sorry. Here . . ." She tried to help him to his feet. "Lean against me and see if you can—"

"Oww!" he cried even louder. "I can't. It hurts too much. You'll have to get somebody to—"

Suddenly there was a low, distant growl. It sounded part animal and part . . . well,

Becka couldn't tell. It was mixed with another sound—a silent, whooshing noise.

"What's that?" Scott said, his eyes wide and suddenly alarmed.

Rebecca wished she had a good answer. She didn't. "I—I don't know." She rose to her feet and searched the field. "I can't see anything but sugarcane."

The sound grew louder, and Rebecca felt her pulse kick into high gear. Whatever it was, it was moving. And by the sound of things, it was moving toward them.

Once again, Scott tried to stand, but it was no use. As soon as he put any weight on his ankle, it gave out and he toppled back to the ground.

The noise was closing in.

"Becka . . ." There was no missing the fear in her brother's voice.

Rebecca reached down for him, fighting off the fear that was sweeping over her. She had no idea what was coming at them, but she knew lying down, unable to move, was no way for her brother to meet it.

She tried pulling him forward, but he was too heavy.

The cane just a few yards in front of them began cracking and splintering.

"Becka!"

Suddenly it exploded through the stalks.

It was big and red. And heading directly for them.

"What is it?" Scott cried.

"I don't know!"

"Becka!"

She reached under his arms, trying to pull him to the side, to get him out of the way.

And still it bore down, ripping cane just a few yards in front of them and devouring it with giant, red jaws.

"Run!" Scott shouted at her. "Get out of here!"

The afternoon sun caught a sharp, shiny blade coming directly toward them, tearing out cane only feet away.

"Get out of here!" Scott yelled at her.

She pulled harder, but it was no use.

"Beck—"

She finally looked up. The giant blade hovered over her and was coming down fast. She screamed and gave one last tug, moving her brother only a foot before tumbling backward. The blade came down.

"Your leg!" Becka screamed. "Your—"

Scott tucked and rolled just as the blade chomped down, missing his flesh by inches.

The threshing machine roared past them, slicing a great swath of cut sugarcane in its path.

Becka couldn't see the driver, but as the

machine passed, she could read a name crudely painted on the back. It was in big black letters. Originally, it had read "BIG SWEET'S CANE KILLER." But over the years some of the letters had been covered by dirt and grime.

Now it read "BIG SWEET CAN KILL."

2

$\mathcal{S}$ara sat in front
of the cracked dresser mirror. Carefully she
outlined her lips with dark lip liner before
applying a deep burgundy shade of lipstick.
So far, she could have been any teenage girl
applying any makeup.

So far.

Next she picked up a medium-sized paintbrush, dipped it in bloodred paint, and drew a streak across her left cheek. She did the same with the right.

Then came the blue. Jagged lines, like small lightning bolts, painted above each eye.

And finally the green. This time she covered her entire chin and the lower part of her neck. At last Sara put down the brush and admired her handiwork. She was very pleased.

~

An hour after their encounter with the threshing machine, Scott sat in Aunt Myrna's best easy chair with his ankle packed in ice. He quietly watched a baseball game on television and poked at some potato chips on his plate.

Rebecca sat nearby thinking how strange it was for her brother to be so silent. Normally he'd be milking his injury for all it was worth, getting people to wait on him hand and foot. But he'd hardly said a word.

Even Mom noticed. When Becka had gone into the kitchen to get a refill on her lemonade, Mom had asked, "Why don't you talk to your brother? He seems so blue."

"What am I supposed to say?"

"It's not so much what you say," Mom replied. "It's your attitude. Just be there for him. You're a team now. If one of you is down, the other should try to help him up."

Rebecca shrugged, poured her lemonade, and strolled back into the living room.

"So," she said, trying to sound casual, "it's almost nine; think we should give Z a try?"

Scott glanced at his watch. "Yeah, I guess."

"Scotty?" She plopped down on the footrest directly between him and the TV. "What's wrong?"

"Hey, you're blocking my view. Move."

"Not until you tell me what's eating you."

"Becka . . ."

"Talk to me."

"Beck."

"I mean it."

He let out a sigh of exasperation.

"Is it the threshing machine with Big Sweet's name on it?"

He shook his head and glanced away. "That's only part of it." She continued to wait, and after a moment he continued. "I'm scared, Beck. This time I'm really nervous."

Becka bit her lip. It was one thing for her to be nervous, but Scotty? As far as she knew her little brother wasn't afraid of anything.

"First our plane almost crashes, then my ankle gets twisted, then we nearly get turned into hamburger by some crazed farm machinery—all this and we haven't even talked to the girl yet."

Rebecca swallowed and tried to keep her voice even. "So you think they're all related?"

"Don't you?"

Becka answered slowly and carefully. "I think someone or something doesn't want us here, that's for sure. And I think whatever it is is very powerful."

Scott nodded in silent agreement.

For a long moment neither said a word. Finally Scott reached for the laptop computer he'd borrowed from a friend and turned it on. He'd already rigged it up to Aunt Myrna's phone line. Now it was simply a matter of dialing Z up on the Internet.

Neither of them knew who Z was or why he had taken such an interest in them. Nor did they understand how he could know so many little things about their lives. Personal things. Things that no one else would know. At times it was almost like he could read their minds. Then there was his knowledge about the occult. On more than one occasion he had gotten them out of jams with knowledge only some kind of expert would have.

Of course they'd tried to track Z down, to find out who he was or where he lived. But each time they tried, their attempts were foiled. Whoever this Z was, he was very clever—and very, very secretive.

"We're in luck," Scott said as he stared at the screen. "He's on line, waiting."

Becka moved in closer to look.

Good evening, Scott, Rebecca. Sorry about the scare on the airplane.

Rebecca fought off a shudder. It was just that type of knowledge that unnerved her about Z.

Scott was already typing his comeback:

How did you know about the plane?

Z didn't answer. But that was no big surprise. He never explained how he knew what he knew. Instead, other words began to form on the screen.

Before you contact Sara Thomas, you should be aware of the facts on voodoo.

Scott and Becka threw each other a glance. It was typical of Z to get right to the heart of the matter.

Like many superstitions, much of voodoo's power comes from the belief people give it. Often too much credit is given to it, and it is blamed for every bad thing that happens.

Scott typed back:

Are you telling us it's all just superstition?

Z's response came quickly:

Not always. In many cases demonic activity can
feed off the fear and superstition voodoo
engenders. Regardless, it is important to
remember that as Christians, the only power
voodoo—or any evil—holds over you is the
power you give it because of your fear.
Do not forget this.

Rebecca stared at the screen as Scott
began typing another question:

Where did voodoo come from?

Voodoo is a combination of African magic and
rituals from the Catholic missionaries. The term
comes from the West African word *vodun*
and the creole French word *vaudau*, both of which
mean "spirit." Ceremonies consist of singing,
drumming, and praying to the dead, whom
they call the *loa*.

Rebecca leaned over to her brother. "Ask
about Sara. Where is she? How do we find
her?"

But before Scott could type the words,
Z answered the question.

Sara Thomas works at the Sorrento library on
Saturdays. Contact her there. It is a 20-minute
bus ride from your aunt's house. Remember,
people usually become part of voodoo to try
to get control of their life. They use black magic
and curses to seek protection from the
supernatural or to get power over others.
They are usually more deluded than evil, but that
doesn't mean they aren't dangerous,
so be careful. Good night.

Scott immediately began typing.

Wait. Don't go yet. We need to know more.

At first they thought he'd logged off. But
after a moment, the final comment appeared:

I must go. You've been trained. You have the
Word, and you have your Lord. The only power
voodoo has over you is the power you give it.
Your tools are prayer and faith. If you remember
these, you will be victorious. Should trouble arise,
seek help from the local pastor.
Good luck and good-bye.
Z

"Good-bye!" Scott turned to his sister in panic. "What's he mean 'good-bye'?"

"I guess—" Becka took a deep breath— "I guess he means we're on our own."

Scott spun back to the computer. "No way. Not this time. Not here."

Z . . . Z, are you there? Z, answer me. . . .

The two waited silently for an answer. But there was none. Z had signed off.

"Great," Scott said, "just great. He sends us all the way out here, then just leaves us on our own." In anger he reached down and snapped off the computer.

Becka ventured a thought. "If Z says we can do it, then maybe—"

"We can't do this," Scott interrupted, "not on our own. You know what we've been through, and we haven't even met this . . . this Sara chick. We're going to need some help. Lots of it."

Rebecca agreed. "He said if we get into trouble we should contact a local pastor."

"A local pastor?" Scott repeated. "What local pastor? We're out here in the middle of hicksville! What would any pastor out here know?"

"Excuse me?" It was Aunt Myrna poking

her head in from the kitchen. "Did you children say you were looking for a pastor?"

Scott and Rebecca exchanged glances.

"I go to the church over in Sorrento. Maybe you'd like to meet my pastor? He has a tiny little church right next to the park."

"Uh, yeah, well thanks, Aunt Myrna," Scott said, doing his best to sound polite. "We'll sure give that some thought."

"That would be nice. I'm sure Pastor Barchett would be able to help you," she said with a smile as she disappeared back into the kitchen.

"Sorrento?" Rebecca repeated. "Did she say 'Sorrento'?"

"Yeah . . .

"Isn't that where Z—"

Scott finished the sentence, "—said Sara was working."

The two traded nervous looks. Was it just coincidence, or had the mysterious Z given them more information than they'd thought?

"We'll try again tomorrow night," Scott ventured. "Maybe he'll be back on-line tomorrow."

Becka nodded, but she had her doubts. Even now she suspected this encounter was going to be different from the others. Different and far more dangerous.

~

In the darkness, the drums pounded.

Doomba-Doomba-Doom. Doomba-Doomba-Doom.

Sara pushed her way through the branches toward the sound. For the hundredth time she wondered if she should go back home. Something inside nagged at her that this was wrong. Very wrong. But each time she thought of turning back, she remembered Ronnie Fitzgerald and John Noey. Their voices, their merciless taunts. No. It had been going on too long. It was time to stop it.

Now.

Doomba-Doomba-Doom. Doomba-Doomba-Doom.

The drums grew louder; she was getting closer.

Sara had been to voodoo ceremonies before, but only the public ones, never the secret rites. These secret ceremonies were held out here in secluded places and known only to members of the cult . . . and to those about to be initiated.

That last phrase stuck in her mind. *Those about to be initiated.* Sara felt her heart beating harder, almost in rhythm with the drums.

Doomba-Doomba-Doom. Doomba-Doomba-Doom.

Through the leaves, she could see the glimmer of a fire. She had found them. They had not given her directions but simply told her to follow the sound of the drums.

She had.

Doomba-Doomba-Doom. Doomba-Doomba-Doom.

She forced herself to go forward, her legs weak and trembling with fear. She knew the stories. She knew what voodoo could do to you. But she also knew what it could do for you. How it could protect you from the others, from the Ronnie Fitzgeralds and John Noeys of the world.

She continued through the brush.

Now she was close enough to see the people dancing about the fire. Some moved in perfect rhythm to the drums. Others darted about, convulsing and writhing like wild animals.

She reached the edge of the clearing. This was her last chance to turn back.

She took a deep, unsteady breath, clutched the small cloth doll around her neck, and entered the clearing.

~

"Scott. Scotty, wake up!"

It was his sister's voice, but it was coming from a long, long way away.

"Scotty, you're dreaming! Scotty, wake up!"

Suddenly he bolted upright. It took a

moment to get his bearings, to realize he'd fallen asleep in the hammock on the porch.

"You OK?" Becka asked. "It sounded like you were having a nightmare."

Scott frowned hard, trying to remember. "Yeah . . . I don't . . . it was screaming. In my dream some sort of animal or something was screaming and—"

Doomba-Doomba-Doom.

He froze. "What's that?"

Doomba-Doomba-Doom. Doomba-Doomba-Doom.

The screen door creaked loudly, and Aunt Myrna stepped onto the porch carrying two glasses of lemonade. "You kids want a cold drink?"

"Aunt Myrna, what's that noise?"

She paused to listen. "Oh," she said, handing out the glasses. "It's them."

"Them?" Becka asked.

"Yes. Big Sweet and his group. They have a voodoo ceremony 'most every night this time of year. You'll get used to the drums after a while."

Scott and Rebecca exchanged glances, both knowing that they would never get used to it.

"Oh, Rebecca?" Aunt Myrna stood at the door, ready to go in. "Did Lukey, you know, our goat—did he follow you out into the cane fields today?"

"No, I don't think so," Rebecca answered. "Why?"

"Oh, no reason," Aunt Myrna said, running her hands through her hair. It was long and gray and beautiful. "It's just . . . well, I guess he's run off again. Can't seem to find him anywhere. Well—" she forced a smile and headed back into the house—"I'm sure he'll turn up."

The door slammed shut behind her, but Scott barely noticed. He was feeling very sick.

"Scotty, what's wrong?" Becka asked. "Are you OK?"

He nodded. When he spoke, his voice was strangely hoarse. "The screaming . . . in my dream?"

"Yeah . . ."

The drums were growing louder now. *Doomba-Doomba-Doom. Doomba-Doomba-Doom.*

"What about it?" Rebecca asked.

"It wasn't a person or anything like that. I remember now; it was an animal."

"An animal?"

Scott nodded. "And it wasn't screaming, it was bleating . . . 'cause it was being slaughtered."

"Bleating?" Becka repeated.

"Yeah, you know . . . like a goat."

The great conch horn sounded, sending its haunting echo throughout the woods.

3

$\mathcal{T}$he morning air
was so fresh and beautiful that Rebecca
almost forgot their purpose, let alone the
danger that surrounded them.

Almost.

The weather forecast promised that rain
would move in later that day, but for now
everything smelled warm and moist and full

of life. Becka especially loved the flowers. They were her passion, her weakness. They always had been. And as she and Scott headed down Aunt Myrna's long driveway to the main road, a gentle breeze stirred and brought half a dozen different fragrances to her.

Scott's ankle was much better. He limped only slightly as they approached the mailbox and began the wait for the bus to Sorrento.

Unfortunately, when the old broken-down vehicle finally appeared, it was belching out more smoke than Mom had created the last time she tried to barbecue. The metal beast screeched to a halt before them, and, as they boarded and headed to the back, any fragrance of flowers was blotted out by the smell of diesel oil and exhaust fumes.

The gears ground loudly, and the bus started lumbering down the road. Soon they passed a large potato field, then a group of run-down shacks. Dirty-faced children in ragged clothes ran all around the yards.

"Look how they're dressed," Rebecca said.

Scott nodded. "And check out their shoes."

Becka looked. "They don't have any."

"Exactly."

Rebecca nodded. "I read that voodoo is most widespread among the poor. Like Z said, it's a way for them to try to gain some control over their lives."

Scott grunted. "Doesn't look like it's working too well."

Rebecca watched a young mother rushing to pick up a dirt-smeared child who had fallen near the ditch. The little one didn't appear hurt, but the mother carefully soothed and cuddled him, tenderly holding him in her arms. Rebecca sighed. "They're people, Scotty. Just like you, just like me."

Scott nodded. It was a lot tougher to look down your nose at someone when you knew it could be you.

Suddenly there was a loud explosion.

"What was that?" Becka cried.

"A blown tire," Scott guessed as he grabbed the seat in front of him and held on.

Had the bus been a newer model, it might have held onto the road, but being old and decrepit, the bus went into a tailspin, its back end, where Becka and Scott sat, skidding around into the oncoming traffic.

The two looked out their window and saw that they were hurtling directly toward a tractor. The tractor driver turned hard, but the bus kept coming at it, brakes screaming and screeching as its tires smoldered from the friction with the road.

At last they skidded to a stop only a few

feet from the tractor, but it wasn't over yet.
The bus started tipping. Becka let out a
scream, certain they were going over, when
suddenly it stopped and righted itself back
up with a mighty thud.

"Sorry 'bout that folks," the driver called
back. "Everyone OK?"

Other than arriving in Sorrento an hour
and a half late (it took the bus driver that
long to find his tools and fix the tire),
Rebecca and Scott were fine. Well, not
exactly fine. Narrowly escaping a plane
crash, nearly being chopped by a thresher,
and now surviving a bus accident—all within
the first twenty-four hours of their arrival—
had taken its toll.

"That does it," Scott said as he stormed off
the bus and over to a small park. "I'm not
going anywhere the rest of the time we're
here."

"Scotty."

"Say what you want, Beck, but something's
after us. Somebody's definitely put some sort
of curse on us."

Becka took a moment to quiet her own
fears, then tried to explain. "Remember
what Z said? Even if it is a curse, even if it is
real, the only fear we have is the fear we give
it. We have to trust that God—"

But Scott was in no mood for reason. "I

think we should turn right around and go back to California."

She knew he had a point. Something was definitely going on. If whoever—or *what*ever— it was wanted to scare them, it was doing a pretty good job. Still, Z had never been wrong before.

She looked up to see Scott heading across the road. "Hey," she called, "where are you going?"

Scott pointed to the large building directly in front of them. "Z said this Sara babe worked at the library, right?" He motioned ahead of him. "Well, there's the library."

Becka crossed the road and joined him. "Listen," she said as they headed up the steps, "better let me do the talking." It wasn't that she wanted to be the one who spoke to Sara. Far from it. She just knew from experience that Scott was in no mood to be overly sensitive, which meant he'd probably offend everyone in his path.

They opened the library door and stepped in. She led the way to the front desk where an older woman was checking out books. "Excuse me," Becka said, "we're look- ing for Sara Thomas. Is she here?"

The older woman smiled and nodded toward two young girls who were putting books on the shelves.

One girl looked fairly normal. The other one had ratted hair with the tips died purple. She wore a black leather jacket with small chains attached to the pockets.

Rebecca took a deep breath. "Well, here goes."

They walked across the room straight to the purple-haired girl.

"Can I help you?" the girl asked.

"Uh, yes," Rebecca began. "This is probably going to sound a little crazy to you, but a friend of ours on the Internet, you know, someone we talk to by computer . . . anyway, his name is Z, and he asked us to visit you, to try to help you through some sort of voodoo thing."

The purple-haired girl made a face. "Some sort of what?"

Rebecca tried again. "Your voodoo thing. We have some experience with the occult and . . ."

"Voodoo?" The girl looked at Rebecca like she had a screw loose. "My voodoo thing? What are you, a whacko? I don't have any voodoo thing."

"But aren't you . . . aren't you Sara Thomas?"

The girl snorted and shook her head. "No. My name is Stacy. This is Sara Thomas."

With great embarrassment, Rebecca

turned to face the other girl—the "normal" looking one—who now stood glaring at her.

"Nice job, Sis," Scott muttered quietly.

"I'm sorry," Rebecca stuttered. "I . . . I didn't mean . . ."

The purple-haired girl nodded and went back to her shelves as Rebecca turned to Sara. "Hello." She smiled self-consciously. "You're Sara?"

Sara Thomas nodded. "Yes." Her voice was cold. "And you are?"

"I'm Rebecca Williams, and this is my brother, Scott. We're here from California to—"

"Yes, I heard," Sara cut her off. "You're here to help me deal with my 'voodoo thing.'"

Rebecca tried to snicker, hoping that Sara would join in and they could laugh off the whole silly thing. But Sara wasn't laughing. She wasn't even smiling. Rebecca was forced to continue. "Yes, I'm sorry about that. . . . I, uh—"

"Listen," Sara cut her off again. "I don't know you, and I don't know anyone on any computer net. I don't even have a computer, and I certainly don't know anyone named Z. And what's more, I don't need your help. I don't *want* your help. And I think you'd better go now." That said, Sara turned back to her books.

Rebecca stood for a long moment staring at Sara's back, trying to think of something to say. Finally she cleared her throat. "Look, I'm very sorry. I didn't mean any harm."

Without turning to her, Sara said, "Go. Would you just go, please."

"Listen." Scott stepped forward. The tone of his voice was not happy. "We didn't come all the way to Louisiana just to—"

"Never mind," Rebecca interrupted quickly. "We've, uh, we've bothered these girls long enough. We should go."

"Yeah, but—"

"Let's go." She took Scott's arm and started turning him toward the door. It was only then that she caught sight of something that sent a chill through her. She hadn't noticed it before, but Sara was now fingering something hanging on a chain around her neck. A small cloth doll.

A doll that looked very similar to the ones the witch doctors used in Brazil.

They were halfway down the library steps when Scott let out an exasperated sigh. "So tell me, could we have messed that up any worse?"

"We just got off on the wrong foot," Becka answered. "That's all."

"Well, she doesn't want our help. I think she made that pretty clear."

Becka nodded and was about to speak when something else caught her eye. Across the road was the small park and beside that was a tiny little church. "Is that the church Aunt Myrna was talking about?"

Scott followed her gaze and shrugged. "I guess. She said it was next to a park."

Becka nodded and started for it.

"Becka . . ."

"Come on. We've got an hour before the bus leaves."

A reluctant Scott followed. He was limping a bit more, and it was obvious his ankle was acting up, but he joined his sister anyway as they approached the church.

They knocked on the door. The pastor was not there. Instead, an elderly lady answered and directed them to the parsonage next door.

They crossed to a small house and noticed that part of the porch stairs had rotted out. It had also been a long time since the building had seen a paintbrush.

Rebecca knocked on the door, but there was no answer. She tried again with similar results. Then one final time.

Nothing.

They started back down the steps when the door suddenly opened, and a small, frail old man appeared. "May I help you?"

"Oh—" Rebecca turned. "We thought no one was home."

The old man smiled. "No, I'm home, but I'm slow. It takes me a while to get to the door."

"We're looking for Pastor Barchett," Scott said.

The old man nodded. "That's me."

"My name is Rebecca Williams, and this is my brother, Scott. We're here visiting Myrna Carmen. She's my mother's cousin."

The old man looked confused. "Who?"

Scott shot a glance at Rebecca as if to say, "Here we go again."

"Myrna Carmen," Rebecca repeated. "She attends your church."

"She's been a member here for like a zillion years," Scott added.

"Oh . . . Myrna." The pastor broke into a grin. "My goodness, yes. So you're Myrna's . . . what did you say?"

"Cousins," Rebecca repeated.

"Ah yes, of course."

"Anyway, we wondered if we could have a few moments of your time."

Pastor Barchett stepped back from the

door and graciously waved them in. "Of course, of course."

Inside, the house was small and well kept . . . except for a cat box that needed to be changed.

Pretending not to notice the odor, Rebecca said, "What a nice house you have."

"One of the ladies from the church comes in every few days and cleans it," the pastor said as he closed the door. "All I have to do is pick up after myself and . . ." He trailed off, forgetting what the other thing was until he noticed Scott's upturned nose. "And change the cat litter, that's it! Sorry about the smell. I forget because the old nose ain't what she used to be. Would you two like some tea?"

Scott shook his head to Becka, and she took the cue. "No, thanks."

Pastor Barchett motioned for them to sit on the sofa. He took a seat across from them. "So . . . how can I help you?"

Becka leaned forward. "Pastor, do you know much about voodoo?"

"I should hope so." The old man's eyes sparkled with a bit of life. "With a church in the heart of Ascension Parish here on the bayou, I'd better know a thing or two."

Rebecca's eyes widened. "Did you say Ascension Parish?"

"Why, yes." The old man nodded. "You know Louisiana is divided into parishes. It's like counties in other states. And this parish is called Ascension."

Becka and Scott exchanged glances. They'd had numerous encounters with the occult through a New Age bookstore back home called the Ascension Bookstore.

"Now tell me, what do you want to know about voodoo, child?" Pastor Barchett asked.

Rebecca told him everything. How Z had sent them to help Sara Thomas. About their experiences with the occult in California. She even described the necklace Sara was wearing.

The old pastor leaned back in his chair, closed his eyes, and thought for a long moment.

Then the moment became longer.

And longer still . . .

Finally, Scott whispered to his sister, "I think he fell asleep."

At the sound of Scott's voice, the old man's eyes popped opened. "I think I have your answer."

"You do?" they both exclaimed at the same time. They leaned forward so as not to miss a single word of wisdom he was about to speak.

The old man hesitated just a moment and then answered, "Pray."

Scott and Becka blinked. They remained silent, waiting for the rest of the answer. But there was nothing else.

"Pray?" Scott said. "That's it? Just pray?"

The pastor nodded. "And believe. Pray that God will show Sara the error of her ways, that she will repent. And believe that he has sent you for a purpose that will not be thwarted."

Scott and Becka glanced at one another in exasperation. Another dead end.

Once outside, it was Becka's turn to show disgust. "Pray?" she said. "Pray?? We could've done that at home. We could have done that in California."

"*And* believe," Scott snorted, shaking his head. "Don't forget believe. It's just the same pat answer we've heard a million times before. I told you no pastor around here would know what was going on."

Rebecca nodded. She knew it was good advice—nothing wrong with praying and believing—but she had to agree that it was pretty much a formula answer and not very helpful in their particular situation.

"Hey, there she is!"

Becka looked up to see Scott pointing toward Sara Thomas. She was leaving the library and heading down the street.

"Come on," Becka said.

"What?"

Rebecca started forward. Before she could admit defeat, she had to try one last time.

"Sara, Sara . . . wait up."

The girl looked up in surprise—and then annoyance. "What do you want?" she demanded as Becka arrived at her side.

"I, uh—I thought maybe, you know, if you were going to lunch, maybe we could sort of treat you."

"You don't think I can afford lunch?"

Becka faltered. "No, that's not it. I just, well, it's sort of, you know, to make up for getting off . . ." the words were coming harder now, "on the wrong . . . foot. . . ."

For a brief second something softened in Sara's eyes. Like she appreciated the thought, like she really wanted to talk—but suddenly she reached for her stomach and doubled over.

"Hey," Scott said, moving to her side, "are you all right?"

"Get away from me. Both of you!"

Rebecca was taken aback. "Sara, are you sure you're—"

"Leave me alone!" She reached out and

shoved Becka away. Hard. So hard that Becka stumbled back, falling against a lightpost. That hurt a bit but not enough to stop her from heading toward the girl again until—

"I'm warning you." Sara was still doubled over and gasping for breath. "If you don't stay away from me, the next time . . . the next time you'll really get hurt." Then, struggling to stand up straight, she turned and started running down the street.

"Sara!" Becka called after her. "Sara, come back. . . ."

But she didn't stop.

Slowly Becka turned to Scott. The look on his face said he was thinking the exact thing she was. What did Sara mean: "The next time you'll really get hurt"?

Becka knew. It was one of two things. Either the bruise she'd received from the lightpost or . . .

Or Sara Thomas was aware of everything that had been happening to them—the near accidents . . . the near-fatal accidents. If they were really someone's attempts to hurt Becka and Scotty, then they'd failed. But not "the next time."

"The next time you'll really get hurt."

Becka could feel an icy chill creep over her body. All morning she had been fighting the fear, trying to keep it at bay. But now it flooded in, and she didn't feel strong enough to stop it. The plane, the thresher, the bus. These were more than coincidences. Scott was right; something was happening. Something was pursuing them. Something more powerful and evil than they had ever encountered before. And if they didn't back off, if they didn't stop now, it could destroy them.

"Beck . . . Beck, you all right?"

She met her brother's concerned gaze and tried to smile, but she couldn't. "Let's get out of here," she whispered. The words echoed in her head: *"The next time you'll really get hurt."* "Let's get out of here now."

4

The trip back to Aunt Myrna's was sad. It was one of the few times Scott and Becka had ever admitted defeat. They knew they'd lost. Not only did Sara not want their help but whatever power she was caught up in was far too powerful for them to battle. Z had overestimated their strength. This they could not fight. And if they tried, they knew they would be seriously injured.

Becka wondered why it was different this time. Why they felt so powerless, so overwhelmed. Maybe they were missing something . . . but when she tried to think it through, Sara's ominous words mocked her.

"The next time you'll really get hurt."

When they arrived back at the farm, John Garrett was waiting to take them on the tour he had promised. But things had changed considerably in the last twenty-four hours, and neither Scott nor Rebecca was particularly thrilled about the idea.

Scott was able to beg off, making some excuse about his ankle. And, as much as Becka wanted to find her own reason not to go, part of her knew the walk would do her good.

Besides, she would no longer be in danger. It was over. They were no longer pursuing Sara. Evil had won. And now as long as they didn't bother it, it wouldn't bother them. The war was over, and peace had been declared. A peace that left Sara as its victim.

The thought bothered Becka, but there was nothing she could do now. She pushed it out of her mind as she followed John past the sugarcane and into the woods.

The place was breathtaking. The low, flat

swamplands had been molded by river waters for thousand of years. Vegetation grew wildly, engulfing and enclosing everything in dim, leafy vaulted chambers. As she followed John Garrett deeper into the foliage, she almost felt as though she were entering an inner sanctum where the sun was an intruder. Plants grew everywhere. Mosses, vines, trees, air plants, water plants, algae, ferns. Everything had life.

And the flowers, they smelled richer in here than anywhere she'd ever been before.

Rebecca felt as though she were in a holy place, a great cathedral of nature, where speaking was forbidden. She stopped for a moment and took a deep breath. "It's . . . beautiful," she whispered. "Beyond beautiful."

John sat down on a nearby log. "Always is. Some people get used to it, I suppose, but not me. Every time I come here, I feel like I did the first time I saw it."

Rebecca nodded. In the distance she heard a rumbling. "Is that thunder?"

"Could be. Kinda feels like it." He looked up toward the trees to see the leaves starting to shimmer and blow. "Suppose we better get you back. It don't last long, but in these parts when in rains, it rains."

"Oh, not yet," Becka protested. "It's so

beautiful; can't we stay just a few more minutes?"

John shrugged. "If you don't mind gettin' wet."

There was another rumble. Closer this time.

"I don't mind."

"Me neither." John grinned. "Nothing like a good shower to wash away your cares, to make you feel alive."

Rebecca nodded. She needed that more than he knew. She looked up and breathed in deeply. Everything about this place made her feel free, alive. Soon she found herself grinning.

"What?" John asked.

"Nothing."

"No, tell me."

"It's just . . . all this beauty makes me . . . I don't know . . . it helps make me more aware of . . . God. Of how powerful he is, how much he loves us."

John broke into an easy smile. "Me, too. Guess that's why I never got too caught up in all that voodoo stuff we were talking about yesterday."

The word *voodoo* brought reality crashing back into Becka's mind. Poor Sara. She would never experience this freedom; she would never taste and enjoy this love. The image of Sara, frightened and alone, fingering the doll around her neck, would not leave Becka's thoughts.

"John?"

"Yes?"

"What does it mean when someone wears a small cloth doll around their neck?"

There was another rumble. Much closer. She looked up. The branches overhead were starting to sway in the wind.

"Might mean nothing." John stood up and started down the path. Becka followed. "But 'round here, that's what an initiate does."

"An initiate?"

"Someone newly admitted to the cult."

Rebecca's heart sank heavier.

A gentle tapping began as drops of water struck the leaves overhead. Soon it was dripping through the canopy in little streams. But it didn't matter. Becka had volunteered to be soaked, and soaked she would be.

The deeper they went into the woods, the thicker the vegetation became, until at one point, the swamp on either side of them was covered from bank to bank with plants. It reminded Becka of a beautiful, jade green blanket.

"Oh, look!" She pointed to a patch of vivid pink flowers. Even in the downpour they seemed to shimmer and glow with light. "What are those called?"

"Got me." John shrugged. "Lots of 'em around back in here."

"They are so beautiful." She took a step or two toward them until John swung out and grabbed her arm. "Be careful."

She looked to him quizzically until he pointed to the green carpet she was about to step on. He stuck his toe into it to show that it was actually water. "Don't want to go in there. Lotsa critters you don't want to be tangling with."

Becka nodded her thanks and looked back over to the flowers. Too bad. They were so beautiful.

John turned and continued leading her down the path.

Once again thoughts of Sara flooded Becka's mind, until a clap of thunder struck so close that Becka jumped. The rain came down even harder. Becka tilted her head back and let it pour over her face. It was refreshing. Exhilarating.

But still, there was Sara.

"John," she shouted over the pounding rain. "Do you know a girl named Sara Thomas?"

John shook his head. "Don't think so."

"I think she might be part of Big Sweet's—"

"Shhh!" John cut her off.

Surprised, Rebecca looked over to him.

He resumed speaking but was barely discernible over the pouring water. "I don't know nobody, and you shouldn't be talking about Big Sweet in here."

Lightning flashed, followed by an immediate explosion of thunder, so loud it made Becka's ears ring.

"You see that over there?" John pointed to something in the woods.

Becka peered through the rain, but the downpour was too heavy to make out anything.

But John kept his hand outstretched, and she continued to stare until finally, through the rain, she saw two bald cypress trees rising into the air.

"I see a couple of trees," she shouted.

"Between them," he yelled. "Look between them!"

Ever so faintly through the sheets of falling water, Becka caught a glimpse of something.

"Is it a cabin?" she shouted.

John Garrett nodded. "That's Big Sweet's place. I never go farther than this."

Rebecca looked at him. There was no missing the concern in his eyes. She turned back to peer through the rain. There was another flash of lightning, and for the briefest second she saw the cabin.

Suddenly she felt very cold, very wet—and very frightened.

Over at Sorrento the rain was just beginning to come down. But the baseball coach wasn't about to let a little water stop his boys from practice.

It must have seemed strange to see Sara Thomas sitting by herself up in the bleachers, no umbrella, the only one sitting in the rain to watch. But Sara had important business to attend to.

Behind the backstop, John Noey swung hard at a pitch and connected. The ball sailed high over the pitcher's head and deep into center field.

"Nice cut, Noey," Coach yelled. "Nice cut."

On the mound the pitcher took another windup and delivered another fastball. This time John sent it into left field, even farther than the last one. At sixteen, John was big for his age and easily the best hitter on Sorrento High's team.

In the stands, Sara, who was growing wetter by the second, reached into her purse and pulled out a doll. This one was also made of cloth but was much larger than the one she wore around her neck.

And it was wearing a baseball uniform.

John Noey stepped out of the batter's box, wiped his bat on a towel, then scuffed his shoes on the ground the way he'd seen the pros do. Noey was cocky, to be sure, but it was more than that. Being a star athlete in high school had given him a brash machismo usually found in much older boys.

Stepping back into the box, he nodded to the pitcher.

Sara held the doll in her left hand while she dug in her purse with the other. For a second she panicked, thinking she'd lost it. But then she felt it and pulled out a large hat pin.

Noey stood confidently as the pitcher wound up to deliver another fastball.

In the stands Sara began chanting something, quietly, over and over. She placed the doll beside her on the bleacher. The chant grew louder. She raised the hat pin high. Then, at the peak of her chant, she jammed the pin hard into the doll's head.

The ball had left the pitcher's hand. It was coming in hard and high. Water dribbled from John's cap, and he blinked once, taking his eye off the speeding ball—but that was all it took. He didn't see it suddenly veer up and inside. He tried to move, to duck, but he was too late. The ball crashed into his forehead at seventy-four miles an hour.

John Noey collapsed, falling face forward into the mud.

Players raced to him. The coaches pushed and shoved to get to him. But Noey was going nowhere. He was unconscious. Maybe for good.

Sara Thomas smiled. "Home run," she whispered, feeling the rush of power sweep over her. Revenge was sweet. But she wasn't finished.

Not by a long shot.

~

Rebecca knew she was going to get yelled at for staying out in the rain. Her soaked clothes and the chilly wind from the storm could prove a powerful combination and make anyone sick. In fact, when she sloshed through the family room and up the stairs, even Scotty rolled his eyes at her foolishness.

After a hot shower and a change into dry clothes, she joined her brother down at the computer. "Any word from Z?" she asked.

Scott shook his head. "Not a thing." He reached over, shut off the computer, and let out a long, slow sigh. "We blew it, Beck. It's over."

Becka nodded sadly.

"Whatever's been happening to us is way out of our league. We've run into stuff more powerful than we can handle. I mean, it's one thing to deal with supposed ghosts and Ouija boards. But how do we deal with something that can drop a plane out of the sky or turn a bus into a whirling dervish? And now even Z's flaking out on us."

"Problems?"

At the quiet question, the two glanced up and found Mom standing in the doorway of the family room. She'd just finished helping Aunt Myrna with the dishes and had come to join her children.

When neither of them answered her question, she plopped down on the sofa and tried again. "Scotty says this is the toughest case you've had."

"You've got that right," Becka said. "For starters, the girl we're supposed to be helping, Sara Thomas—she doesn't even want our help."

Mom nodded. "That's hard. But not unusual."

"What do you mean?"

"Lots of times the people who need help are the ones who don't want it. Like Julie. Or Krissi."

Becka stared at her mother. She was right! How had she forgotten the resistance they'd met anytime they'd tried to help someone who was caught up in the occult?

Mom went on. "What did Z say?"

"That's another thing," Scott said. "He won't talk to us. He sends us out here all on our own and then just abandons us."

"He didn't give you any advice?"

"Just that we're suppose to believe and not give in to our fears."

"And he mentioned the pastor," Becka reminded him.

"Oh yeah." Scott's tone was filled with scorn. "The pastor. Z said the local pastor would help."

"And?"

"The old-timer can barely remember his name, let alone tell us what to do. All he could come up with was, 'Pray and believe.'" He shook his head. "Can you believe that? Just 'pray and believe.'"

Mom frowned slightly. "Sounds like pretty solid advice."

"Well, yeah, I mean, I know," Scott said, blinking. "But we've only heard it a million times."

"So you've done it already, then?"

Scotty blinked again. "Done it?"

Mom tilted her head. "Prayed."

Scott and Rebecca looked at each other, then at their mother.

"Uh, well, no . . ." Scott admitted hesitantly.

"Not exactly," Becka added. "We've been

. . . busy." But even as she said it, she knew it
was a lame excuse.

Mom nodded. "Well, I've got time now, if
you're interested."

"For what?"

"Well, to pray, of course."

"Here?" Becka asked. "Now?"

"Can you think of a better time?"

The brother and sister glanced at each
other a little sheepishly, and Becka laughed
softly. She couldn't believe it. In all their
hurry and determination to be the great
teen ghostbusters, she and Scott had forgotten a couple of very important ingredients:
to pray and believe.

Ingredients they'd been reminded of by
an ancient pastor who had trouble staying
awake. She grinned. Maybe the man wasn't
as out of it as they'd thought.

"Sure," Becka said, and Scott nodded.
They moved to the couch, bowed their
heads, and began to pray with Mom.

In the dream, Sara was wearing a wedding
veil. She looked beautiful all in white, and
her face glowed with anticipation as she
walked down the aisle toward her future
husband. Though the groom's back was to
her, she knew he would be perfect.

Everything in this dream was perfect.

There was her mother in the first pew, healthy and vibrant like she had been before she got sick. And here by her side was her father, handsome and proud, like he was before he started drinking.

Everything was just the way she'd always hoped it would be. . . .

Until the groom turned around.

A thick red horn protruded from his forehead, and his face was black and blistered as if it had been charred. But it was the eyes that terrified her most. Huge and black. Staring at them was like looking into deep wells. Wells that had no bottom. Only horror. Deep, dark, everlasting horror.

Sara woke up screaming.

She fell back against the pillow, her chest heaving with ragged breaths, and closed her eyes in an effort to go back to sleep. She couldn't. The dreams had been coming more and more frequently. And with them, the nausea. The same nausea she had felt when talking with the two kids from California that morning.

There was only one way to take her mind off the nausea. And the monster. To think back to the beautiful woman she had seen in the dream. To remember how things had been when her mother was alive, before she got sick and died, before her father buried his grief in alcohol . . . before her life had been ripped out from under her.

Hot tears sprang to her eyes. That's how it always was when she thought about the past. But that was OK because sooner or later the crying would tire her out and she would fall asleep. That's how it worked most nights. She hoped it would tonight.

5

ara Thomas knew that Ronnie Fitzgerald would show up at Janet Baylor's sweet-sixteen party because Janet was the most popular girl in school. Sara was surprised to have even been invited, but apparently Janet had decided to invite the entire sophomore class, even the poor Raggedy Ann who everyone ignored.

Sara spent most of the evening off by herself, secretly spying on Ronnie and watching for the right moment.

Earlier she had hollowed out a large candle and buried a lock of Ronnie's hair in the wax along with a slip of paper on which she had written "Worst Luck" and "Ronnie Fitzgerald" seven times. She had then dug a small hole in a field near Ronnie's house in a place where the moonlight would shine on it. She buried the bottom half of the candle in the hole, lit the wick, and gone home.

All of this was according to the instructions the *hungan* had given her. The hardest part had been getting the lock of hair, but even that proved easier than she had expected. All she had done was sit behind him on the bus, and when he leaned his head back, she snipped off a piece.

He never even knew.

Many of the kids at the party had started changing into their swimsuits and jumping into the Baylors' large pool. Ronnie wasn't out there yet, but Sara knew he soon would be. He wouldn't miss a chance to show off his body and his diving skills.

Sara moved closer to the patio doors so she could get a better view of the crowd around the pool. It was then that she heard someone crying. Cautiously she peered around the kitchen door and listened to an older woman talking with Mrs. Baylor.

"They say they don't know . . . he might never wake up," the older woman sobbed.

"Try not to worry, Mrs. Noey. John's in good hands," Mrs. Baylor said. "It's the best hospital in the county."

Sara felt a pang of guilt jab into her gut. John Noey's mother. It had to be. He was still in a coma, and the doctors were saying that he might never come out of it.

"I know he's not always a good boy," Mrs. Noey said, wiping her nose. "But he lost his papa when he was little, you know, and he never got over it. He loved his papa so much. . . . He's been angry at the world ever since. But he's always helped take care of me and his little sister. He's like a daddy to little Gina. She was just a baby when Ralph died, and John's tried hard to make it up to her."

Sara's head spun, and her heart filled with remorse. She'd never given a thought to John Noey's family and how they might feel. She had never considered how losing him might affect their lives.

Sara drifted away from the kitchen, trying hard not to hear Mrs. Noey's sobs. Out of the corner of her eye she saw Ronnie Fitzger-

ald bouncing high on the diving board—
and her eyes widened in horror.

*Oh, no! I don't want this now! Not after what
happened to John. No! Don't let—!*

But it happened. Ronnie—the perfect
athlete, the expert diver—lost his footing
on a high jump and flipped backward
instead of forward. Thrown back onto the
board, he struck his head with a hard
thump.

The blow was so solid that Sara heard it
through the patio glass. Nearly sick with guilt
and horror, she watched the unconscious
Ronnie roll off the board and strike his head
again on the side of the pool before tumbling
into the water.

People rushed to his aid. Sara heard someone say something about not moving him,
and a couple of girls were screaming over
the blood.

She couldn't look. All she could do was
turn and walk away. And wonder if she would
ever stop feeling completely, totally awful.

~

The following morning Rebecca was sick.
The wind and rain from yesterday afternoon
had taken their toll. She was coming down
with something; she was sure of it.

"You look terrible," Scott said as she arrived at the breakfast table.

She sniffed and mumbled something about his looking in a mirror once in a while himself.

"Are you feeling all right, dear?" Aunt Myrna asked as she shoved a plate of eggs, a thick slice of ham, and grits under Becka's nose.

"It's just a little cold," Becka mumbled through a sniffle. It wasn't exactly a lie, but it wasn't the truth either. Whatever she was coming down with was going to be bad. One good clue was the way her stomach was turning at the smell of the food. Or the way her head was already starting to ache.

"So what are we going to do our next three days off?" Scott asked as he started on his second bowl of grits.

"I think—" Becka sniffed again—"I think we should give Sara one last chance."

"Beck . . ." Scott started to protest.

"I know, I know. We said it was over, but don't you think we should at least give her one more try? And this time maybe do it the right way?"

Scott gave her a look. "You mean like the pastor said, with prayer and believing?"

Becka nodded. "That's what Z said, too, remember?"

Scott gave a loud sigh. It was a sound she recognized—one that said he was really put out with her. But it also said that he'd have to go along with her, and they both knew why: She was right.

~

There were many dancers at the ceremony, but Sara danced the wildest of all. Her movements were frenzied, driven, as though she were stomping all her troubles into the earth.

Suddenly she couldn't breathe. She choked, gasping for air. The other dancers came to a stop and stared as she gagged, pointing at her throat, begging for help.

No one moved.

She dropped to her knees, motioning frantically until everything started to grow fuzzy and white. Then whiter and whiter until she crumpled to the ground.

A large black man rose from an old wicker chair that looked like some sort of throne. Sara watched hazily as he came to kneel over her, placing his fingers on her neck as though feeling for a pulse.

At last he looked up and spoke. "Sara is dead. She defied the gods. She has been struck down."

Sara wanted to argue, to disagree, but she

could not seem to open her mouth. Or move her body.

Suddenly she felt herself being lifted up. But now she was no longer herself. Somehow she had become somebody else.

Now she was John Noey!

She was lying in a hospital bed hearing her mother weep over her. No, not *her* mother. *John Noey's* mother. She tried to move but could not. She could still hear. She could still feel. She knew all that was going on around her, but she could not move.

John Noey could not move.

Hot tears fell onto her arms as the mother began to sob and cry over her.

"I'm sorry," a doctor's voice said, "we've done all we can do."

She felt a sheet being pulled over her face. Dead! John Noey had just been declared dead!

But she was alive! She had to tell them! John Noey was still alive. Only now she wasn't John Noey.

Now she was Ronnie Fitzgerald!

Wires covered her body. Tubes stuck into her nose and mouth—no, *his* nose and mouth. She was alone. All alone. Just the quiet blip of the heart monitor over her head. And the rhythmic sound of the air as it was being pushed in and out of her lungs by a respirator.

Suddenly the heart monitor started blipping irregularly. She panicked, tried to move, but there was nothing she could do. She could feel the heart inside her chest pounding like a jackhammer gone berserk. Then it stopped altogether. So did the blips on the monitor. Now there was nothing but a long, loud whine.

She tried to breathe but couldn't. To scream, but no words would come. She heard people racing around her, someone shouting, "He's flatlining; we're going to lose him!"

Sara was desperate to move, to breathe—she was silently choking, suffocating until—

Sara sat bolt upright, awake and coughing.

When she caught her breath, she glanced around the classroom. More than a few students were staring at her. Several were smirking. She had fallen asleep in class again. Not surprising, since she'd given up sleeping during the night in an effort to stop the dreams. But apparently that didn't matter now.

The dreams were coming during the day, whenever she closed her eyes and started to doze. Day or night, the dreams came.

Sara looked at the clock. It was almost three o'clock. She was anxious to leave. All this time she'd thought revenge on the boys would make her feel better. It didn't. It made her feel worse. The sobs of John's mother, the sound of Ronnie slamming into the board, they just kept echoing in her mind.

But it was more than guilt. Sara was afraid. Now she knew the power of voodoo . . . and she was starting to realize that it could turn back on her if she wasn't careful.

At last the bell sounded. Sara let out a sigh of relief. All day long the school had been getting reports on John's and Ronnie's condition from the hospital. It was all any-one talked about. Both were in comas in Intensive Care. Sara wanted to get away. To go home and cover her head.

To sleep.

These were the only thoughts running through her mind as she headed toward the bus.

"Sara. Excuse me, Sara Thomas?"

Someone was calling her. She turned and saw Rebecca and her brother waiting at the bottom of the steps. *Oh, no,* Sara thought. *They're the last people I want to see.*

Rebecca stepped forward. "Sara, listen, I just want to say something. It may not be any of my business, but if you're messing around with—"

"Then leave, OK?" Sara cut her off. "If it's

none of your business, then take your creepy brother and just—"

"I want to warn you," Rebecca interrupted. "I want to warn you that if you're messing around with voodoo, you could be losing control of your life."

Sara's eyes grew wild. "Why are you trying to hurt me?" she demanded. Her voice grew more shrill. She knew others were listening, but she didn't care. "You want to take away my powers, don't you?"

Becka reached toward her. "Sara—"

"No! I'm warning you for the last time. Leave me alone!"

Now it was Scott's turn. "Listen, we're not trying to hurt you or take away any—"

"You bet you won't! 'Cause I won't let you." Sara reached inside her purse and pulled out the scissors she had used to cut Ronnie's hair. "Get out of my way."

Rebecca froze. "All right, Sara, we'll leave . . . but couldn't we just—"

Suddenly Sara lunged at her. "I warned you!"

Becka jerked backward, lost her footing, and fell hard onto the sidewalk. Sara swooped down at her with the scissors.

"Stop . . . !" Scott tried to block her, but she was too fast.

But instead of stabbing Becka, Sara suddenly cut off a lock of her hair.

Rising to her feet, she shouted, "I curse you. Worst luck will befall you. *Pire* sort! *Pire* chance! *Pire* fortune!" She started backing away. "Worst luck! Worst luck! Worst luck! It will be worse for you than it was for John and Ronnie."

Sara spun around and started running. Her heart pounded in her chest. She had to get away. She knew the magic was about to begin, and she did not want to stay around and watch the two suffer.

~

Scott bent down to his sister and helped her to her feet. "You OK?"

Becka nodded. "Yes, just sort of stunned. She cut my hair."

"I know," Scott said. "Nothing like being cursed to really trash a day. C'mon. I think we'd better get home."

"But the bus to Aunt Myrna's isn't due for another hour."

"I mean *home* home," Scott replied. "Back to California."

By the time they got to the bus stop, Rebecca was feeling a lot worse. Maybe it was the emotion, or maybe it was the fever she knew had been rising steadily all morning.

Whatever the case, at the bus stop Becka had to sit on the bench.

"Can I get you anything?" Scott asked. "A Coke or something?"

She could see he was worried. "Maybe some kind of juice," she said.

"All right. I'll check the store inside the gas station over there. Just wait here."

Rebecca dreaded the bus ride back to Aunt Myrna's. The bumping and bouncing on that old bus would only make her feel worse. She closed her eyes. The throbbing in her head was unbearable.

She opened her eyes and glanced at the abandoned newspaper lying beside her on the bench. It was *The Sorrento Times,* and the headline read: "Second Sorrento High Student in Coma."

Despite her throbbing headache, Becka forced herself to read on. Ronnie Fitzgerald had been injured the night before; John Noey, the day before that. Both boys were in the hospital, barely clinging to life. Both were victims of strange accidents that, according to the paper, "many in the area believe are due to religious rituals."

Suddenly Sara's words came screaming back into her mind: *"It will be worse for you than it was for John and Ronnie."*

Her eyes shifted back to the paper, scanning for the injured boys' names again. There they were. Ronnie Fitzgerald and John Noey.

Rebecca's vision blurred. The trees and people around her started to move. She was worse than she thought. The fever, the headache, the encounter with Sara. And now this.

"It will be worse for you."

Fear continued to grow, consuming her, fogging her thinking.

"Next time you'll really be hurt."

It was the fear that had been piling up since even before they had landed. She tried to focus her eyes, but it was impossible. Now the people, the trees, the buildings were all beginning to spin.

"It will be worse."

She could feel herself growing clammy with icy cold perspiration.

"Worst luck! Worst luck!"

She was going to faint. She knew it.

"I curse you! I curse you!"

She was going to—

Suddenly she felt her body tilt forward. She tried to stop herself but couldn't. A moment later she toppled off the bench and onto the sidewalk.

Rebecca Williams had passed out.

6

When Becka woke up, she found herself lying on the bench with Scott and Pastor Barchett standing over her. "But you'll pray for her, won't you, Pastor?" Scott was asking.

Pastor Barchett nodded. "Of course I will, but you have the authority of prayer also. Curses and spells have no power over Christians unless we give it to them."

Rebecca moved and tried to sit up.

"Beck, you're awake. Are you all right?" Scott asked.

"How are you feeling, my dear?" Pastor Barchett said.

"I feel better, I think," she said, though she was still a little woozy.

"I ran over and got the pastor," Scott explained.

"Maybe you should see a doctor," Pastor Barchett offered.

"I'm all right," Becka said. "It's just . . . well, I haven't felt real good all day. With Sara attacking me, and all that's been happening to us, and then reading in the newspaper about those two Sorrento High boys and their freak accidents . . ."

"Yes," Pastor Barchett nodded. "Both classmates of Sara's, I've heard. I'm afraid it sounds like more than a coincidence to me, too."

"I think I'll be all right now," Rebecca repeated. "Did we miss our bus?"

Scott shook his head. "Should be here any sec. Unless . . ." Suddenly he had an idea and turned to the pastor. "I don't suppose you'd drive us home?"

The old man laughed. "No, they've long since stopped letting me drive a car . . . eyes are bad. But I'm sure I can find someone to take you."

"I'll be fine on the bus," Rebecca assured them. "It's just a short ride. But what should we do about Sara?"

"Keep praying," Pastor Barchett said, *"and believing*. But remember, you can't deliver someone from something if they don't want to be free. They have to want it."

"Well, she's made it pretty clear that she doesn't," Scotty said. "Sounds like Z really missed the boat this time. How could God possibly want us to visit Sara when she doesn't even want to listen?"

"What about Moses and Pharaoh?" Pastor Barchett asked. "God sent Moses, didn't he? What about the prophets? Just because the people didn't listen doesn't mean God didn't send them."

Rebecca leaned forward. She was still feeling a little light-headed, but she wasn't about to admit it. "I think we should give it a couple more days," she said.

"Becka . . ." Scott started to protest.

"Two more days," she repeated.

Pastor Barchett was already nodding in agreement. "And in the meantime, keep praying . . . and believing."

~

By the time they got back to the farm, Scott had to argue with Rebecca to get her to take a nap. "But I feel good now. In fact, I'd like to go for a walk. I want to show you these pretty flowers I saw in the swamp."

"A walk?" Scott exclaimed. "No way. You have to lie down and rest."

"Stop acting like my mother," she snapped. "I feel fine."

"All right," Scott said, "if you won't listen to me, let's talk to Mom and see what she says."

Becka panicked. "No! Don't tell Mom. She'll make me stay in bed for a week."

"Then take a nap."

"If I take a nap, will you walk with me into the woods so we can smell those pink flowers?"

Scott made a face. "Flowers?! What do I care about flowers?"

"There's lots of other stuff, too. It's really cool. Please . . ."

Scott hesitated.

"I'll owe you," she promised.

"All right . . ." Scott finally agreed. "But you have to rest first."

"Will do."

But Rebecca couldn't sleep. She was still a little foggy-headed, and she knew the fever hadn't left. She also knew something else. She knew that although she pretended it wasn't true, her fear of Sara and her powers was still very, very strong. Probably *too* strong.

Then there were the other thoughts. The ones that had been growing more powerful every hour. The thoughts that had been insisting she go into the swamp and smell those incredible pink flowers.

᠕

On Sara Thomas's bedroom dresser was a glass full of those very same pink flowers.

Buried amidst them were the locks of Rebecca's hair.

And underneath the flowers? Underneath the flowers was a live snake.

᠕

An hour later Rebecca and Scott set off for the woods and swamp. Becka couldn't explain it. Even though she still felt weak, finding those flowers, seeing their beautiful color, had become very important. It was like a craving. Something she couldn't stop wanting.

She led the way. For a while they followed the path she and John Garrett had taken. But each time she thought she saw a glimpse of the pink flowers, she veered a little farther off until, before she knew it, they were on a path she'd never seen before. A path surrounded by deep, thick vegetation.

They continued forward until, minutes later, they spotted a good-sized clearing up ahead. It looked like some sort of gathering place where a dozen logs were arranged in a huge circle.

Growing all around the clearing were the pink flowers.

"Wow! Cool place," Scott exclaimed. "You never told me about this."

"I've never seen it before," Becka said. "I must've taken a wrong turn back there."

"What do you think this was?" Scott asked as he started to explore. "An Indian church or something? It looks ancient."

Rebecca barely heard him. Instead, she found herself walking along the logs, stopping every so often to smell one of the flowers. "Aren't they beautiful?"

"What?"

"The flowers. Aren't they beautiful?"

"Yeah. Beautiful. You know, Beck, all you've talked about since we came out here are those flowers."

"They're so beautiful."

"What's the matter with you?" Before she answered, Scott's eyes landed on something else. A large, makeshift altar made of flat gray stones. "Hey, check it out."

They ran to it but suddenly came to a stop.

"Is that red stain what I think it is?" Scott asked.

Rebecca nodded, glancing around. "Don't see any flowers here."

"Beck, I'm pretty sure that's blood. And look here. There's some kind of animal hair sticking to the rock. Something was killed here recently. Somebody's using this place for animal sacrifices." Scott stepped back as the memory of his terrifying dream about the goat came rushing back.

"Let's go look for more flowers," Rebecca said.

Her words pulled Scott from his momentary shock. He looked at his sister long and hard. Something was up, and he was feeling more uneasy by the second. "I think we'd better get you home."

This time Scott took the lead, heading out of the clearing and trying to find the path. But after thirty or so feet, he stopped cold and pointed at something in a nearby ditch. "Look, Beck!"

Rebecca joined him. "More flowers?"

Scott didn't respond. He just stood staring. In the pit was the remains of a slaughtered goat.

"Oh . . . that's terrible," Becka said.

"Guess we know now why Aunt Myrna's

goat hasn't come home," Scott said sadly. "Big Sweet slaughtered him in one of his rituals."

"We should go," Rebecca said.

"You're right," Scott agreed, turning and heading for home.

"No," she shook her head. "We should go and look for more flowers."

Scott spun around to look at Becka. Her face was flushed, her eyes bright and kind of glazed. The unease in the pit of his stomach became full-blown concern—and anger. Something had happened to Becka. And whatever was wrong with his sister was getting worse by the minute. He had to get her out of here. But as he looked around, a deep sinking feeling hit his gut. They were lost. He was sure of it.

"Becka? Beck, I think we'd better pray. I think—"

But when he turned back to her, she was gone.

"Becka!" he shouted, looking around. He began to panic, running first one way, then the other. "Becka!" he shouted again. *Dear God, he prayed, don't let me lose her. Not in here!* "Becka!"

But she was nowhere to be found. Desperately he continued the search. Plants were everywhere. Spanish moss hung down thick in his face. Everything looked the same. He had no idea where he was or if he'd been there before.

"Becka! Bec—"

Then he heard it. Splashing. And he knew as certainly as if he'd seen it happen . . . Rebecca had jumped into the water.

"Becka!"

He followed the sound, racing along a log.

"Becka! Becka!"

At last he saw her. She was up to her neck in the water, a few feet from the shore.

"What are you doing?!" he demanded.

She didn't answer. Instead, she started treading water, moving *away* from him.

"Becka!!"

A moment later he had his answer. She reached out and grabbed a handful of the pink flowers.

"See?" she called. "Flowers."

"Yes . . . very nice." It was all Scott could do to contain himself. "Now if you don't mind, would you hurry up and get out of there? We've got to—"

Suddenly he saw movement in the water. It looked like a log drifting across the swamp. But it was no log. His heart began pounding. It was an alligator. It was an alligator swimming right for his sister!

"More flowers over here," she called, starting to paddle even farther away.

"No, Beck! Come back! Get out of there! Look over your shoulder!"

Rebecca did, but she seemed oblivious to the approaching gator. Its two large, yellow eyes were coming straight toward her, and she didn't seem to see a thing.

"Look, Scotty." She pointed past the gator toward another group of flowers. "More flowers."

Scott was beside himself. "Nooo!" he screamed from the shore. "Look, Beck. I've got flowers here." He scrambled around the shore scooping up flowers wherever he saw them. "See, Beck? I've got bigger ones, prettier ones! See? Right over here!"

Rebecca turned and saw Scott waving his handful of flowers. She smiled and began swimming back to him.

It was too late.

Her pace was no match for the gator, which rapidly closed the distance between them. It would be on her in seconds.

"Oh, God!" Scott cried. "Please save Rebecca. . . . In the name of Jesus please save her; please . . ."

The alligator was only a few feet from her now. Its mouth opened wide, preparing to attack, when suddenly—

BAM! BAM!

The shots cracked through the swamp like thunder.

At first Scott was unsure what had happened. Then he saw the great alligator roll over onto its back and watched as blood appeared in the water. Finally, the creature sank slowly out of sight into the green carpet of water and plants.

There was a crack and rustle of brush. Scott spun to the right to see a huge black man appear. He was carrying a rifle. Perched on his head was a battered straw hat, and he was chewing on a piece of sugarcane.

"It's all right now, missy," he called. "You can take your time comin' back. But you best get outta there soon as possible. This area's got more gators than that old-timer."

Scott could only stare as Rebecca swam toward him. Once again she was smiling.

When she arrived, the big man reached his hand out to help her. "Hello there, missy. Pleased to make your acquaintance. My name is Benjamin, but most folks in these parts call me Big Sweet."

7

*B*ig Sweet contin-
ued to hold out his hand to help Rebecca
from the swamp, but she hesitated, remain-
ing in the chest-deep water.

"Flowers?" she asked.

The big man smiled. "What?"

"She's talking about these," Scott called.
He was about thirty feet away, holding up a

handful of the pink flowers for Big Sweet to see. "She's obsessed with them. That's why she dove into the water. Because of the pink flowers."

Big Sweet nodded as if he understood. "Sounds like she's under some kind of spell."

Confused and growing more angry by the second, Scott crossed toward the man. "Yes, and you did it . . . or one of your people. . . ."

Big Sweet held up his hand. "Whoa, son. Easy. We can talk about all that later. But no matter what you've heard, I am still preferable to another alligator."

"What?"

"We must get this girl out of that water before we have more company."

Scott understood and quickly joined the man. He leaned over the bank and held out the flowers to his sister. "Here they are, Beck. Come and get 'em."

As Rebecca reached for the flowers, Scott and Big Sweet took her arms and pulled her out of the water. She was soaked and dripping with slime.

"Look at your leg," Scott said. "It's bleeding."

"She must've cut it on a briar under the water," Big Sweet said. "You better come over to my cabin and let me clean that wound for you."

"I don't know," Scott said warily. "We should be heading back. Just point the way to Aunt Myrna's house and—"

"Look, son, if I wanted to harm you, you'd already be dead. I could've let that gator eat your friend here and shot you instead. Truth is, I hate shooting gators. Ain't that many more left. And we got plenty of kids. Especially white Yankee kids out messing where they don't belong."

Scott was unsure whether to be terrified or angry, until Big Sweet broke into a big, booming laugh. "Now, c'mon to my place," he said, "and let me dress that wound 'fore your friend winds up with an infection."

Scott nodded. "OK . . . but don't try anything funny."

Big Sweet laughed again, then turned and made his way up a small hill. Scott followed cautiously, taking Rebecca by the hand and leading her carefully.

Big Sweet's cabin lay on the other side of the hill. It looked foreboding on the outside, but once inside, Scott was surprised to see that it was small and cozy. He was also surprised to discover that the man had a wife and two cute little girls who were four and six. In fact, the whole place looked suspiciously normal.

"Why you keep looking around like that?"

Big Sweet asked as he washed the blood off Rebecca's leg. "You expect bats to fly out of the closet?"

Scott almost smiled. "Something like that, I guess. We've never been in a . . ." He stopped in midsentence, unsure of what words to use.

"In a *hungan*'s house?" Big Sweet asked. "Is that what you mean?"

Scott swallowed.

"Well, son, a *hungan* is just like anyone else . . . most of the time." Rebecca sat quietly, playing with her handful of flowers as Big Sweet continued cleaning around the wound. "It's only during the ceremony that the *loa* commune with the *hungan*. Otherwise he's like anyone else."

"How can you say you commune with the dead and call yourself normal?" Scott asked. He knew he was being pretty direct, but after all, this was the top man, the guy in charge.

Big Sweet cocked his head and looked at Scott. "What's a city kid like you know about the *loa*?"

Scott shrugged. "Not much. I just like studying stuff like that."

Big Sweet's thick eyebrows knitted into a frown. "Stuff like what?"

Usually words came easily to Scott, but

now, with Big Sweet staring at him, looking
through him, he wasn't sure how to answer.
"I just . . . like to read about . . . weird stuff."
Scott winced as soon as he had said the
words. Calling someone's religion "weird
stuff" was not too bright, especially if that
someone happened to be the high priest
and was two or three times your size.

Big Sweet's eyes narrowed, and he looked
meaner than ever . . . until he suddenly
broke into the biggest laugh yet. "Weird
stuff." He continued laughing. "Weird stuff.
That's pretty good."

Scott gave Big Sweet half a smile, then
glanced over to Rebecca. She did not say a
word; she was too busy playing with the pink
flowers.

Big Sweet reached for a bottle of alcohol,
poured some onto a wad of cotton, and
warned, "This might sting a bit."

But as he swabbed the cut with alcohol,
Rebecca didn't even react.

Big Sweet shook his head. "That's a powerful curse. May take some doing to break it."

"Ask Sara Thomas," Scott said. "She's the
one who put the curse on her."

Big Sweet was taken aback. "Sara Thomas?
How do you know—" He dropped off, then
shook his head. "I must explain to you what
is happening to Sara Thomas. You know

about the *loa,* the dead spirits. Well, there are two kinds of *loa. Rada loas* and *petro loas.*"

Scott listened uneasily.

"*Rada loas* are good spirits that help a person do good. *Petro loas* are mean spirits that help them do evil."

"What's that got to do with Sara or my sis—"

"Sara Thomas, she's been picked on all her life. She needed something to defend herself, to fight back. That's a *petro loa.* That's what she sought and—" he let out a sigh—"that's what she got. A spirit of revenge."

"So you put a curse on Sara, and Sara put one on my sister."

Big Sweet looked at Scott a moment, then shook his head. "I did not put a curse on Sara. She asked for help; I gave it to her. She got herself a powerful *petro loa,* though. A strong one. I'm afraid Sara's a *loa's cheval* now."

"A what?"

"That means horse, a horse for the spirit to ride. And there is not much she can do until it decides it wants to get off."

"What about my sister?"

Big Sweet thought a moment. "I've got a black root. It can break spells like—"

"I don't want any of your magic," Scott interrupted.

Big Sweet frowned, not understanding.

"She's a Christian," Scott explained. "Curses have no power over Christians."

"So I see . . . ," Big Sweet said, motioning to Becka, who was still playing with the flowers.

Scott faltered. "That is, unless we give you that power, that authority."

Big Sweet sat waiting for more.

Scott continued. "A lot of weird stuff's been happening to us. And Becka's been getting kinda spooked. And now with the fever and all, and Sara pretending to curse her, I guess she just started to give in and believe—"

"So what are you going to do?" Big Sweet interrupted.

Scott swallowed. "I guess . . . pray."

"Pray?"

"Yes."

"Pray? That's it?"

"Well . . . yeah."

Big Sweet folded his arms. "OK, let me see."

"What? Here?" Scott asked.

"I would not be taking her back into the swamp this way. But then again, if you don't think it will work . . ."

Scott quickly rose to the occasion. "Oh, it will work, all right. You bet it will work."

Big Sweet grinned. "Then I am waiting."

With growing determination, Scott pushed

aside his apprehension and reached over for Rebecca's hand. Next he bowed his head and closed his eyes. "Dear Lord . . ." He cleared his throat, still feeling a little self-conscious. "Dear Lord, please break the power of this curse. Please help Becka to see that she doesn't have to be under this or any spell because of what you did for us on the cross. Because you set us free and gave us an even greater power." Scott hesitated. Part of him wanted to make the prayer longer and more dramatic, maybe turn it into a minisermon, but he had said what needed to be said, and that was enough. "In the name of Jesus Christ I ask these things. Amen."

Scott opened his eyes.

Big Sweet sat silent, waiting. "That is it?"

Scott nodded. "That's it."

"No root or balm or potion?"

Scott shook his head. "We don't use that stuff. We don't need it."

Big Sweet turned and stared hard at Rebecca, waiting.

Nothing.

"Missy?" Big Sweet called. "Missy, are you there?"

Then, ever so slowly, Becka turned her head toward him.

Both Scott and Big Sweet held their breath.

At last Rebecca spoke. "Would you like a flower?"

Scott winced. Big Sweet smiled.

Rebecca continued, frowning slightly. "No? Then can I dump them somewhere? I think they're making me sick. I must be allergic to them or something." She looked around the room, blinking in confusion. "Hey, where are we?" She looked down at her soaked clothes. "And how did I get all wet?"

Scott let out a sigh of relief, and Big Sweet laughed his big laugh.

"Hello, missy," the man said. "My name is Big Sweet."

Rebecca turned to Scott, a trace of panic in her voice. "Is he serious?"

Scott nodded. "It's OK. You were out of it for a while, and Big Sweet saved your life. We came here so he could clean that gash on your leg, and, uh, well, I just prayed and broke Sara's curse."

Rebecca leaned back in her chair. She was feeling a little weak. And for good reason. It was all coming back to her now. The cravings, the wanderings, Sara's curse. She reached up and rubbed her neck. It was still stiff from the fever. "Boy, do I feel stupid."

Scott continued. "Big Sweet says Sara is possessed by a violent spirit."

"A *petro loa,*" Big Sweet added. "There are

good spirits and bad spirits that can possess a person and—"

"But possession is wrong," Rebecca interrupted.

Big Sweet looked at her.

She continued. "If there's one thing we've learned over the months, it's that any spirit that possesses someone is not a good spirit."

Big Sweet rubbed his chin. "For a couple of kids, you sure think you know a lot about spirits."

Becka and Scott exchanged glances. If he only knew . . .

Big Sweet continued. "I don't know what you got, but it is clear it has power. Breaking that curse with no roots or potions is mighty strong power."

"Our power doesn't come from something," Scott explained. "It comes from Someone."

Big Sweet eyed him. "All right, then. If you really want to help Sara Thomas, you must come to the ceremony tonight. Her *petro loa* is a dangerous one. I tried talking to it, but it won't listen. I've tried to get its ancestors to talk to me, but—"

"You can't talk to the dead," Becka cut in.

Big Sweet was obviously growing impatient with all the interruptions. "You cannot?

Then who have I been talking to every week all these years?"

Again Scott and Rebecca traded looks.

After a deep breath, Scott finally answered him. "Demons. You have been talking to demons who are using you for their own purposes."

Big Sweet stood up. "You kids give me a big headache. You better head back now. Miss Myrna will be worried."

"And Sara?" Scott asked.

"If you are serious 'bout helping Sara, then you come to our ceremony tonight."

~

Sara was having another nightmare, tossing and turning and groaning. She woke up gasping for air, then jumped out of bed and hurried over to the dresser mirror to stare at her reflection.

She let out a scream.

In the mirror, she saw snakes in her hair. Then they were gone.

She sat and stared at herself. It looked like she had aged several years in the last few days.

Angrily she grabbed the small cloth doll still hanging around her neck and ripped it off, breaking the chain. She threw it on the floor and hurriedly got dressed.

But just before she left the room she walked back over to where the doll lay on the floor. She stared at it a long moment. Then, though it was the last thing she wanted to do, she picked it up and put it in her purse.

She had to. She no longer had a choice.

~

Going to the ceremony was the last thing Rebecca and Scott wanted to do. Especially given Becka's condition and all they'd been through. But they both agreed that it would be their last opportunity to help Sara. And like it or not, that was why they had been sent here in the first place.

Before they left for the encounter, both of them knew they needed to remind themselves of the power God had given them. The events of past days had shaken their trust and weakened their faith. There was only one way to build it back up. They grabbed their Bibles and headed for the porch, where they started rereading some of the sections promising them their authority in Jesus.

"Hey, remember this?" Scott asked as he flipped to a well-worn page and began to read: " 'The Spirit who lives in you is greater than the spirit who lives in the world.' "

"Yeah," Becka sighed, "too bad I forgot

that earlier." She glanced to a page she had found. "Here's another one we'd better not forget. 'These signs will accompany those who believe: They will cast out demons in my name. . . . '"

Scott nodded and read from still another section: " 'If you believe, you will receive whatever you ask for in prayer.' "

"Praying and believing," Becka mused. "Sounds exactly like what Z told us at the very beginning."

"And Aunt Myrna's pastor," Scott added.

Becka shook her head. "Funny how you can hear some stuff so much that pretty soon you don't even pay attention to it."

"Well, we're paying attention now," Scott said as he rose to start getting ready. "Nothing's going to make us back down tonight."

"Scotty?"

"No, sir, we're going to get in there and bust some heads."

"Scotty?"

"Show them they're not messing around with just any—"

"Scotty!"

"What?"

"Before we go, shouldn't we, like, you know, pray first?"

"Oh . . ."

For the first time she could remember,

Becka actually thought she saw her brother blush.

"Yeah, of course." He cleared his throat. "I, uh, I knew that."

She gave him a grin as he sat back down. And there, together, brother and sister bowed their heads to pray for God's protection. They asked God's forgiveness for their wavering and their pride and asked for his wisdom and for the faith to do whatever he wanted. Neither was sure how long the prayer lasted, but that didn't really matter. They continued praying, neither wanting to stop until they were positive the Lord had thoroughly restrengthened them and, most important, until they were positive it was his will for them to even go.

The ceremony was in full swing when Rebecca and Scott arrived. In the center of the clearing a large fire was burning. A dozen dancers, all dressed in colorful costumes, their faces painted different colors, moved slowly around the fire to the beat of the ever-present drums. Most of those gathered were barefoot.

Sara Thomas was nowhere to be seen.

Big Sweet, on the other hand, was. He wore the same battered straw hat and chewed on a piece of sugarcane. He was seated in a big wicker chair that looked more like run-down patio furniture than a seat of honor. Every once in a while, he smiled and waved at Rebecca and Scott from across the sea of dancers.

Finally the drumming stopped.

Big Sweet stood. He began to chant in a language that Rebecca didn't understand but guessed was probably French or Creole. At the end of what seemed to be a prayer, the drums began beating again. This time much faster.

Big Sweet raised his arms to the sky. "I call upon you *Bon Dieu.*" He closed his eyes and waved his arms. "Bring forth the *loa* now to help and guide the people."

He sat down, and the drums began churning out an even faster rhythm.

"I know *loa* means the dead," Rebecca whispered to Scott, "but who is *Bon Dieu* again?"

"He's the most powerful of the gods," Scott whispered back. "Kind of like the supreme ruler."

Most of the dancers moved in the same undulating rhythm as they had before; others began jerking spasmodically, like puppets on a string. A few even threw themselves to the ground and began twitching like bugs in the dirt. One man ran wildly around the circle as fast as he could, screaming hysterically until he collapsed onto the ground from exhaustion.

"This is getting too weird," Scott whispered.

Rebecca nodded. Once again she had that sick feeling in the pit of her stomach that they were in over their heads. But the prayers and the Bible verses they had read still echoed in her heart. She knew she and Scott were exactly where they were called to be. Not only would God protect them, she knew he would also show them what to do.

On the other side of the dancers, she noticed a man whose entire face was painted bright red. He was glaring at them. She nudged her brother. "Do you see that man? The one with the red face?"

Scott looked around. "Nope . . . I see a green-faced man, a guy with orange spiders on his cheek, a woman with a blue star on her forehead and . . . oh, that guy. What's the matter with him?"

The red-faced man started moving toward them, waving his walking stick to clear the dancers out of his way.

Rebecca gulped. "He's coming over here."

Scott shook his head. "No, he's not. He's just heading out to . . . wait. He *is* coming over here."

The red-faced man never took his eyes off them as he pushed and shoved one dancer after another out of the way. When he arrived, he towered over the brother and sister and pointed at them. *"Sama sama tay, sama sama tay!"* he shouted.

A few of the nearby dancers stopped and stared at Rebecca and Scott.

Suddenly the red-faced man leaped high into the air and screamed, *"AIEEEEEEYA!"*

The cry sent chills through Rebecca and Scott, but they held their ground.

The drums stopped beating, and everyone quieted.

"Sama sama tay!" The red-faced man shouted, pointing at them. *"Sama sama tay!"*

The whole group stared now. Rebecca tensed. She waited, silently praying. Others in the group joined in with the red-faced man, chanting, *"Sama sama tay! Sama sama tay!"* They crowded closer around Scott and Rebecca.

"Sama sama tay! Sama sama tay!"

More and more joined in, pushing themselves closer and closer.

"Sama sama tay! Sama sama tay!"

The red-faced man raised his walking stick high into the air.

"Sama sama tay! Sama sama tay! SAMA SAMA TAY! SAMA SAMA TAY!"

Rebecca wanted to bolt, to break through the crowd. She was sure the crazed-faced man intended to crack her and Scott over the head with his stick. But instead of running, she closed her eyes and prayed for all she was worth. She hoped Scott was doing the same.

Suddenly the conch horn sounded.

Everyone froze and turned toward Big Sweet. He blew the giant shell two more times.

The red-faced man was not about to give up. He pointed at Rebecca and Scott and shouted again, *"Sama sama tay!"*

Big Sweet angrily shook his head. "No! No *sama sama tay. Untero tay. Untero my tay!"*

The dancers seemed relieved by what they heard and turned away. But the red-faced man leaned over Rebecca and sniffed her hair.

"No!" Big Sweet shouted again. *"Untero tay. My tay!"*

The red-faced man stepped back. He gave a slight bow in Big Sweet's direction and rejoined the group. The drums began again, and the dancers resumed their gyrations.

"What was *that* all about?" Scott whispered.

As if to answer, Big Sweet called across to them. "That fellow thought you were intruders. Spies, trying to steal our secrets. I told him you were my guests. Potential members to join the group."

"Potential members?" Scott shouted incredulously. "You told him that?"

Big Sweet laughed. "Who knows? The night is young."

Before Scott could respond, a pale girl came out of the brush and entered the ring of dancers.

"Look." Scott pointed. "It's Sara."

Though she was wearing nothing unusual—high school P.E. shorts and a T-shirt—Sara stood out dramatically from the dancers. True enough, most of the others were having some kind of experience, but Sara . . . Sara seemed to be fighting a war. She twisted and contorted one moment, flowed with the rhythm of the drums the next, then contorted again, fighting against something with all her strength.

Slowly Big Sweet stood. This time he shouted out the names of several spirits. Some he called *rada loas*.

The drummers increased their tempo. Big Sweet walked through the dancers until he finally arrived at Sara's side and spoke. "And you, Sara? You are ready for your final rite of initiation into our group?"

Suddenly Sara stopped moving. Her eyes glared up into Big Sweet's face. She tried to shake her head no, but her whole body began to tremble.

Scott leaned over to Becka and whispered. "Look at her eyes. She's scared to death! She's trying to fight this thing."

Scott was right. The girl's eyes were wild and filled with fear as her body shook harder and harder, clearly out of control.

Rebecca rose to her feet. "We have to help her. We have to—"

Animal growls suddenly came from Sara's mouth. Her body twisted and contorted uncontrollably.

Big Sweet tried to embrace her, to hold her, but she pushed him away and flung herself to the ground.

The crowd began to murmur, but Big Sweet raised his hands. "Sara is fighting with her *petro loa* for control of her body. She will tear herself apart unless I can quiet the spirit with the Magic Balm."

"No," Becka called. She started to push her way through the crowd. "Don't—"

But her voice was drowned out as Sara began shrieking, wrestling and rolling in the dirt. Big Sweet signaled two other men for help, and it took all three of them to hold her.

"No!" Becka repeated. "She doesn't need potions, she needs—"

Sara's scream was unearthly, unrecognizable, as Big Sweet applied some special ointment. Then, almost instantly, she quieted. The fit subsided, and she lay perfectly still.

Scott and Rebecca stared.

"I guess he does have power," Scott finally ventured.

But Rebecca wasn't convinced. There was something wrong. She couldn't put her finger on it, but something wasn't right.

The drums began again, and the dancers resumed their actions. Big Sweet turned to Scott and smiled triumphantly. But Rebecca didn't notice. Instead, she approached Sara and knelt down to her. She leaned over and looked. Now she knew what was wrong.

Sara wasn't breathing.

Quickly Becka reached for Sara's neck and felt for her pulse.

There was none.

"She's dead!" Becka cried. "Sara's dead!"

8

Immediately
Rebecca and Scott put their CPR training
to work, Becka blowing air into Sara's
mouth several times and Scott pumping
Sara's chest.

"It's not working," Becka shouted.

"We've gotta keep trying," Scott yelled.

Becka returned to the girl's mouth, and

Scott continued working on the chest. But it was no use.

"Still no response," Becka cried, feeling for Sara's pulse. "We have to get her to the hospital."

Big Sweet offered his beat-up pickup truck, and they quickly loaded Sara into the back. Rebecca and Scott crawled in with her to resume the CPR as Big Sweet sped off.

"I've seen this before," Big Sweet called through the back window. "When the *petro loa* gets violent, the Magic Balm sends the *loa cheval* into a deep sleep. She will wake up OK; I give you my word."

"She's dead!" Rebecca shouted. She could feel her eyes starting to burn with tears. "Don't you get it? She's dead!"

"Don't blame yourself," Scott shouted over the wind. "We did everything we could do. Like Pastor Barchett said, you can't deliver someone if they don't want—"

"But she did!" Rebecca cried, wiping the tears out of her eyes. "She wanted to be delivered. I could see it in her eyes. She was fighting for control when that demon thing killed her!"

Minutes later Big Sweet skidded the pickup into the emergency entrance of Sorrento's hospital. Scott threw down the gate while Big Sweet scooped Sara up and raced inside with her.

An attendant helped him get her onto a gurney, and Becka gave the nurse all the information she knew as they wheeled Sara into another room.

Time passed. Rebecca paced. Eventually she looked up to see Scott approaching.

"Where's Big Sweet?" she asked.

"He had to get back to the ceremony."

"He what?" Becka felt herself growing angry.

"Yeah, he said the people needed him and, uh . . ."

"And what?" Rebecca demanded.

"And that, well, that Sara would be all right."

Becka couldn't believe what she was hearing. She turned to a chair and slumped into it. Her fever was rising again; she could tell by the chills. It was rising, and it was draining what little energy she had left. She was angry, she was scared, and she was reaching the point of total exhaustion.

Scott sat beside her. "You going to be OK?"

"I don't know." Once again she could feel the hot tears springing to her eyes. She tried to blink them back but couldn't. Finally she looked up at him. "Somebody's just died, Scotty. That's never happened to us before."

Scott nodded.

"Where's all our power? All those verses that say we're supposed to have the victory?"

Scott had to look away. When he spoke, his voice was thick and faint. "I don't know."

"I'm scared, Scotty."

"Don't say that," he said. "Fear is a weapon of the enemy. If we believe he has the power instead of God, then he can beat us."

"He's already beaten us."

"Don't say—"

"She's dead, Scott! We lost! She's dead!"

"Excuse me?"

They both looked up to see a nervous older nurse approach. "Are you the ones who brought Sara Thomas in?"

"Yes," Rebecca said, already preparing herself for the worst.

"Well . . ." The nurse took a breath. "She's gone."

Rebecca nodded. "I know. We were just hoping you could do something to—"

"No, you misunderstand," the nurse said. "She's not gone as in dead. She's gone as in she got up and left."

"She what?!"

"I don't know where she is. I don't know what happened. One minute I had no life signs, and then . . . she just sat up and said she was fine."

"How's that possible?" Scott asked.

"I couldn't believe it myself. I raced to get the doctor and when we got back into the room, she was . . . gone."

Rebecca and Scott continued to stare, not believing their ears.

~

The late-night streets of Sorrento were barren as Sara Thomas wandered them. For several minutes she had stood outside the hospital. The same hospital where John Noey and Ronnie Fitzgerald were still fighting for their lives.

She felt terrible for them . . . and for herself.

Her identity was ebbing away. She knew it was true. *I've used the power of voodoo,* she thought, *and now I must serve its power.*

The irony almost made her laugh, but she knew she must not. The *petro loa* in her demanded full attention. If she let down her guard, even for a moment, it would take over again. And then even what little was left of Sara Thomas could vanish.

Completely.

Big Sweet had been right. He had told her that she could not resist the *petro loa* on her own. If she tried to stand against the spirit, it would make her insane, it would take complete control of her, maybe even kill her.

She remembered other bits of information and counsel he had given her.

"Can you heal me of the *petro loa?*" she had asked hopefully.

Big Sweet had only shaken his head. "No, I cannot do that. But I can teach you how to stay healthy while you learn its ways."

"Learn its ways?" she had asked. "What do you mean?"

"The *loa* may leave you in time, Sara, but for now, you must learn to live with it. Learn when it is awake and when it sleeps. Learn what it requires of you. Then you will be able to use what is left for yourself."

"You're asking me to let the spirit rule so that it might let me have a little of my life back?" she had asked incredulously.

Big Sweet had nodded. "I know no other way. When my father studied with Marie Leveau, we knew a man who had been a *loa cheval* for forty years. In the daytime he was a wonderful man. He used to take me fishing, and he often brought little candies to us kids. But my father warned us to stay away from the man at night because that was when his *petro loa* came out, and he was very violent. It took five men to hold him down. But his life was not a total loss. He had his days."

Unable to think of this any longer, Sara

turned from the hospital and headed down the street. She didn't care where or for how long. She just had to get away.

Soon she found herself passing the old church near the library where she worked. Unable to explain her attraction to it, she came to a stop in front of the church, then turned and moved up the stairs. She hesitated, then reached out and tried the door.

It was open.

It was eerie inside the church at this hour. It was lit only by a small lamp near the front and a few votive candles.

Sara took another step inside and suddenly began to feel very nauseous. Holding her stomach, she turned to go, when she was suddenly startled by the presence of an old man.

He was thin, and his white hair caught the moonlight. He was kneeling in the back pew praying. She hoped he hadn't noticed her, but suddenly he looked up, directly into her eyes.

"Sara?" the old man stammered. It was obvious he was as surprised as she was.

For an instant Sara was frozen with shock. Who was this man? How could he know her name? The nausea increased, and she backed away toward the door.

The old man rose unsteadily to his feet.

"I am Pastor Barchett. Just now I was praying for you. Please, won't you—"

Sara spun around to the door. The nausea was worse. She had to get out. Still, something inside was crying. Begging her to stay. With great effort she forced herself to turn back around and face the old man.

"Help me . . ." she cried. "Please . . . help—"

Suddenly her mouth slammed shut. She felt herself spinning around, saw her arm reaching for the door and throwing it open.

"Sara, please—"

She could barely hear him over the laughter filling her head. Taunting laughter that was not hers. She felt herself moving, her body heading outside and down the steps. There was no stopping now—the *loa* was in charge again.

And it was forcing her to return to the ceremony.

~

"I say we go back," Scott insisted.

"Scotty . . ."

"Listen," Becka's brother was up on his feet, pacing. "We've done everything the Bible's said, right?"

"Well, yeah, but—"

"We've prayed and believed, right? Just

like Z suggested, just like that pastor guy said."

"I know that. But . . ."

"But what?"

"Scotty, she nearly died."

"But she didn't. Come on, Beck, where's your faith?"

"My faith is . . ." Rebecca took a long, deep breath and slowly let it out. The fever was up again, and she was fighting off the chills. "I'd like to go, Scotty. But I'm . . . I've got nothing left."

Her brother looked at her.

"I'm sorry." She shook her head and pulled in her legs to try to keep herself warm. "I'm wiped out. I'm . . . I'm sorry."

Scott looked at her for a long moment. But instead of making her feel guilty, he quietly knelt beside her. "You're right. I don't know what I was thinking. It's been rough on you. Way rougher than on me."

"I'm sorry," she repeated. "I feel like a total failure, but I just don't even think I could—"

"That's OK. You just stay here."

Becka looked up. "What?"

"You stay here at the hospital and call Mom and Aunt Myrna to pick you up."

"You're not going alone?"

He was already rising to his feet. "Beck, we came here to do a job."

"You saw the power there; you know what can—"

"I know, I know. We've been beat up more than a few times on this one. We've lost a few battles. But the war isn't over. Not yet." He turned and started for the door.

"Scott—"

" 'If you believe, you will receive whatever you ask for in prayer.' "

She struggled to rise to her feet. "I know that, but—"

He turned back to her one last time. "Give Mom a call. Have her pick you up. And then the two of you pray for me."

"Scotty?"

"Pray a lot."

"You can't go there by yoursel—"

But he was already out the door. It slammed shut behind him.

Rebecca stood, frustrated. Frustrated and exhausted. She closed her eyes, trying to think what to do. Scott must not go back to the ceremony alone. And yet—

"Excuse me, are you Sara Thomas's friend?"

Becka looked up to see a young doctor entering the room. She nodded.

"We'd taken a sample of Sara's blood and were running some tests . . ."

"Yes?"

"It seems her blood contained trace amounts of a rare poison."

"Poison?"

"Yes . . . curare. It's from a tree that grows in South America. When you apply it externally like a salve on the skin, it sometimes renders the victim unconscious. It can slow down the heartbeat to where life signs are very hard to detect."

Rebecca couldn't believe what she was hearing. "You mean it makes you look like you're dead."

"Yes, and if applied externally in small amounts, its effects last less than an hour . . . which explains Sara's return to consciousness. Unfortunately, if it's taken internally, or if the subject receives too much over a short period of time . . . well . . ." He hesitated.

"Please, go ahead," Becka insisted.

"I don't know where your friend would have contact with something like this, but she should be careful. If she's exposed to it again too soon . . . it will kill her."

Becka stood stunned, her mind reeling. The first time, Sara had been lucky. But if she was heading back to the ceremony, and if Big Sweet applied the poison again . . .

"Listen, you look a little pale," the doctor said as he approached Becka. "Maybe we should take your temperature and—"

Becka started for the door. Of course he was right. She felt terrible. But Sara's life was in danger. And if somebody didn't tell her, if somebody didn't warn Big Sweet and Scotty . . .

"No, I'm fine," she lied. "Thank you."

"Are you sure?" the doctor called.

But Becka was already out the door. As the doctor's question followed her, she shook her head. She wasn't sure. She wasn't sure she could make it. If she did, she wasn't sure she could help. But she *was* sure of one thing. She had to try.

"Help me," she prayed as she headed down the street, across town toward the distant swamp. "Please, Lord, give me the strength I need."

9

*D*oomba-Doomba-
Doom. Doomba-Doomba-Doom.

The drums echoed through the swamp.
Rebecca was fine as long as she could follow
their sound. The moon was three-quarters
full and bright enough to allow her to make
her way through the thick undergrowth and
woods.

Just as long as she could hear the drums.

She was still shivering. It was either her rising fever, the night air, or the resurgence of her fear. Probably all three.

Doomba-Doomba-Doom. Doomba-Doomba-Doom.

For the most part she avoided falling into the water or running face first into branches, both strong possibilities when stumbling through the bayou at night.

Doomba-Doomba-Doom. Doomba-Doomba-Doom.

But she still had the drums to direct her. She still had—

Suddenly, they stopped.

Becka hesitated, then stopped. She strained to hear the slightest sound, the slightest clue. There was nothing. She had never been in this part of the swamp, and without the drums she knew she was lost.

Panic gripped her. She wanted to run, to scream for help, to plow through the swamp and its treacherous waters, to keep running and running—running to get out of the swamp, running to help her brother, running to prevent Big Sweet from reapplying his Magic Balm.

She knew it was fear. The same fear that had been her enemy throughout the trip. Fear on the plane, fear of the thresher, fear of Sara's curse . . .

"No!" she shouted to no one in particular. "I am not afraid!"

The fear subsided but only for a moment.

"NO!" she repeated. But the fear left and returned even faster. So she did the only thing she could think of. She began quoting Bible verses, from those she'd learned as a child to those she and Scotty had read earlier that evening.

" 'The Spirit who lives in you is greater than the spirit who lives in the world. . . . If you believe, you will receive whatever you ask for in prayer. . . . Perfect love expels all fear. . . .' " As she continued, the fear slowly faded. A peace settled over her, as though filling her head with God's truth left no room for fear's lies.

As the peace came, so did a quiet logic and rationale. She decided to sit on a nearby log and wait patiently for the drums to resume.

But what if the drums never started again? What if the ceremony was over? What if Sara was already—

Once again Becka thought of the verses, and once again a gentle peace settled over her.

As she sat on the log, she could hear the soft rhythmic sound of crickets. The buzz of a thousand tiny insects. Frogs calling from deep within the swamp. The place was a virtual symphony of nature.

Yes, God was good. Very good.

There was the hoot of an owl from a distant tree. The splash of some small animal going into the water. And the rattle of a snake . . .

A snake! Rebecca froze.

Maybe she was wrong. Maybe it was something else.

No, there it was again. It was a snake's rattle, and it was closer than before.

Rebecca squinted as she peered at the ground around her feet, looking for some movement.

There was nothing.

The rattle had sounded as if it had come from the left side, so she started to rise, preparing to run to the right.

Then she heard the rattle again.

This time it came from the right.

Ever so slowly, Rebecca stood up from the log. Then, out of the corner of her eye she saw it. Something slithering along the ground. She turned fast to the left.

Too fast.

Her foot caught a snag on the log. She felt herself toppling forward; she tried to shift but only overcompensated and threw herself backward, arms flailing as she tried to regain her balance.

It did no good.

She landed exactly where she didn't want to be—less than a yard from the snake.

The rattler raised itself up, preparing to strike.

"Please, Jesus," she cried, "make it go away!"

As if in answer, the snake rattled even more menacingly and reared its head back. Becka could see its silver black eyes glaring at her in the moonlight. She closed her eyes, expecting the worst. Then, just as suddenly as it had risen, the snake lowered back to the ground and slithered off in the opposite direction.

Rebecca watched, amazed at how loudly her heart was pounding . . . until she realized it wasn't her heart, but the drums. They had resumed beating.

She stood up, took a deep breath to steady herself, then headed toward the sound.

◊

Big Sweet nodded slightly when Scott entered the clearing and found a place in the outside circle. The dancers had already worked themselves into a frenzy by chanting, whirling, singing, screaming.

Immediately Scott spotted Sara. She was moving with the same jerky movements as before, twisting, contorting, and crying out in a strange language. Her voice was unnaturally deep and husky. She had all the symptoms. Scott knew the signs.

Sara was possessed.

The time for action had come. He rose to his feet and started toward her.

The showdown was about to begin.

Big Sweet also rose from his wicker chair. He wasn't sure what Scott was about to do, but he wasn't taking any chances. The *petro loa* in Sara Thomas was powerful. If it was cast out of Sara, there was no telling how many of his people it would attack. He would not let them be injured.

Carefully he reached into the leather bag that hung from the back of his chair. He extracted a small tin container. In it was the same potion he had used earlier that night. A potion from the strychnos tree. The tree was originally from South America, but Big Sweet's father had replanted it in the bayou when Big Sweet was a small boy. Its resin was blackish and brittle, but when mixed with certain roots, it turned into a dark brown salve. It was his Magic Balm.

Scott continued toward Sara. He was ten

feet away when she suddenly spun around and stared right through him.

Scott had seen this cold, lifeless stare before. He knew these were not Sara's eyes. They were the eyes of what Big Sweet called the *petro loa*. Scott knew it by another name.

The demon stared at him cautiously.

Scott came to a stop. Slowly, he raised his right hand. The battle was about to begin.

Suddenly the demon snatched a walking stick from a nearby dancer and twirled around. He was so fast he caught Scott off guard, slamming the stick into the boy's face and knocking him to the ground as blood spurted from his nose.

The demon lunged at him, raising Sara's arm for another blow.

"No!" Big Sweet shouted. He held the open container in his left hand. The fingers of his right hand were covered with a white powder to help shield him from the effects of the Magic Balm. "I speak to the *petro loa* occupying Sara Thomas. You shall not hurt this boy."

Sara's head nodded in agreement, but the nodding grew more rapid and exaggerated until it was obvious the spirit was mocking Big Sweet.

Scott raised himself to his knees, trying to

clear his head. But instantly the *petro loa* swung the big stick down hard on him.

Scott cried out in pain.

Big Sweet motioned to his men, and they moved in. Three of them leaped on Sara from behind while Big Sweet dug his hand into the tin of Magic Balm, preparing to smear it on her.

She struggled and almost broke free. A fourth man joined the fray, and they were finally able to hold her down. Big Sweet approached and raised his hand, intending to smear the balm on her arm.

"Stop!" It was Becka. She was running into the clearing. "Don't touch her with that. It's poison!"

Big Sweet looked at her. "I must use the Magic Balm to quiet the *petro loa*," he shouted. "It will not kill. Only make the *loa* sleep. You saw yourself."

Rebecca strode quickly toward them. "It will kill!"

Big Sweet frowned.

Becka continued. "I spoke to the doctor at the hospital, and he said the more you use, the more dangerous it is. You've already used some to knock her unconscious. He said that if you use more too soon it will kill her."

"But I must quiet the *petro loa* before he

brings harm to her or to one of my people. Look at your brother."

"I'm OK," Scott said, struggling to his feet. "It's just a nosebleed."

Sara's body once again writhed, and the four men struggled to hold her down.

Big Sweet started toward her. "I must quiet the *petro loa*."

"I will quiet the *petro loa*," Rebecca shouted.

All eyes turned to her. She looked to Scott who slowly rose to his feet, nodding to her in encouragement.

She took a deep breath. Then turning to face Sara, Becka called out in a loud voice: "In the name of Jesus Christ of Nazareth, I command you to come out of her!"

There was no movement. Nothing.

Rebecca moved closer. "You, demon who occupies Sara Thomas, you come out of her now. In the name of Jesus Christ. I order it!"

Suddenly, with superhuman strength, Sara tossed aside the four men who held her. She rose to face Becka, practically snarling. "Who are you?" Sara's mouth moved but the voice was deep and guttural. "Why do you force your will on others?"

"It doesn't matter who I am," Rebecca said with confidence. "I am not the one forcing my will. You are. Now, be gone in the name of Jesus Christ—"

"What makes you think—"

Rebecca cut the demon's words short with a sharp motion of her hand. She knew all too well that demons argued only to stall or weaken a believer's faith. She would allow neither. She couldn't afford to. "I said go in the name of Jesus Christ. Now!"

Sara's body tensed as if charged by electricity. She let out a loud, ghastly cry; then she went limp, dropping to the ground.

All who watched gasped. Many began to murmur, wondering at the power they had just witnessed. Rebecca didn't notice their wide-eyed wonder. She was focused entirely upon Sara. She moved to kneel beside the still girl and tenderly touched her arm.

"Sara," she said. "Sara, it's OK now. Sara . . ."

Sara's eyes snapped open, and before Becka could defend herself, the girl kicked her with all her might.

Becka cried out, tumbling backward to the ground.

"There's more than one of them!" Scott yelled.

Sara leaped to her feet and started for Becka.

"Stop!" Scott shouted. "Enough trickery! I command you to stop!"

Sara froze, then slowly, with great menace in her stance and expression, turned to face him. But faith was surging through Scott. He was not about to be intimidated, not when he knew who truly held the power in this situation. "We command you in the name of Jesus Christ to be gone. We cast you into the pit."

Becka had struggled back to her feet and approached from the other side. "Be gone. All of you! We cast all of you out of Sara and into the sea of fire. In the name of Jesus Christ, go!"

Sara's body began to tremble, her face twisting and contorting grotesquely. The onlookers backed away. Some even turned and ran.

Sara threw her head back and shrieked a long, agonizing wail, more animal than human. It echoed through the trees and across the swamp—and then she finally collapsed to the ground, unconscious.

Rebecca and Scott looked at each other. They knew she was clean this time, that all of the demons had left. They approached and knelt at Sara's side.

"Sara . . ." Rebecca said. "Sara?"

A moment later, the girl's eyes flickered, then opened.

"Are you all right?" Rebecca asked.

Sara nodded. "I think . . ." Her voice was hoarse and dry, and she licked her lips painfully. She looked up at Becka, her eyes weary but hopeful. "He's gone, isn't he? And his friends . . . they're all gone."

Rebecca nodded. "Yes."

Relief crossed Sara's face, and for the first time she seemed to relax.

"Is this what you want?" Becka asked. "To be free of them?"

Sara nodded. "Yes . . . yes . . . of course." Then her forehead wrinkled. "But what about the boys—what about John and Ronnie?"

"Are you sorry you hurt them?" Scott asked.

"Yes." There was no mistaking the sadness in Sara's voice. "I am very sorry."

Rebecca smiled warmly. "Then why don't you pray for them with us?"

"Pray? To who?"

"To the very person who gave us the power to cast out the *petro loa*," Scott answered her.

Sara looked at him; then slowly she nodded.

Rebecca and Scott bowed their heads. After a moment, Sara followed suit.

"Dear Jesus," Becka began, "we ask your forgiveness for what Sara has done."

"Forgive me," Sara murmured.

"And we ask that you heal those boys. Make them whole again."

Sara nodded, tears forming in her eyes.

"And, Lord," Becka continued, "please reveal your love to Sara. Help her know your truth."

Sara was beginning to sob now.

Rebecca grew quiet, continuing to pray silently for several moments. When they finished, Rebecca looked up at Big Sweet, who had been watching the encounter with the demon and the following prayer with astonishment. "The Magic Balm is dangerous," she said.

Big Sweet nodded. "I will not use it again. I only did as I was taught. The *petro loa* was bad."

"It was a demon," Scott explained. "Not the spirit of someone who died, but a fallen angel. A demon."

Big Sweet sighed. "Perhaps. I do not know your ways. They are not the ways my father taught me. But they are not bad ways."

"We believe in one God," Rebecca explained, "the *Bon Dieu* who rules over everything."

"*Bon Dieu.*" Big Sweet nodded in agreement. "That I understand. But he does not communicate with us."

"He does through his Son," Rebecca said. "And it was the power of his Son that you saw demonstrated here tonight."

Big Sweet met her eyes. "His Son?"

Both Becka and Scott nodded.

"And a name—this Son has a name?"

"That's right," Becka said. "His name is Jesus. Jesus Christ."

10

*R*ebecca and Scott invited Sara back to Aunt Myrna's that night, and the three of them talked long into the morning.

"I'm really sorry for the way I treated you," Sara said. "I—I was just afraid after what I did to John and Ronnie, that somebody would try to . . ." She dropped off, then shook her head and resumed. "It seems funny now, but this last week it's like all these things happened to someone else . . . like it wasn't even me."

"In a way it wasn't," Rebecca explained. "The more you got involved with voodoo, the more you lost yourself."

Sara shuddered at the thought. "I'm just glad it's finally over."

Rebecca and Scott exchanged looks.

"Actually," Scott cleared his throat. "It isn't over . . . at least not yet. But it can be."

Sara looked up concerned. "What do you mean?"

"Those evil spirits, they'll try to come back."

Sara sank deeper into the chair. "Oh, no! I knew they would."

Scott nodded. "The Bible says they will come back if you haven't filled up the vacancy they left."

"Filled the vacancy?" Sara asked.

Becka explained. "The only thing that can protect you from evil spirits returning is accepting Jesus Christ as your Lord and Savior. Once that happens, once he's in your heart, then when they try to return, you'll have the authority to stop them."

"Are you serious?" Sara asked. "I can have that authority?"

Becka and Scott nodded.

"Well, what do I have to do?"

Carefully Becka and Scott explained how Jesus had died on the cross to forgive Sara of her sins. They told her about his being raised from the dead and that all she had to do was ask him to forgive her and take the punishment for those sins.

"That's it?" Sara asked.

"That's only half," Scott said. "You also need to let him be your Lord."

"Lord?"

"Yeah, you know—like your boss. The boss of your whole life."

"You mean him being the boss instead of me?"

Scott nodded. "No offense, but so far it hasn't turned out too great with you in charge."

Sara nodded, almost smiling. "Then that's what I want to do," she said. "Give your Jesus all of my life. I've had lots of trouble. I don't want any more."

"It isn't so much that you won't have trouble," Rebecca corrected. "It's just that Jesus will always be there to show you the way through that trouble."

Tears welled up in Sara's eyes. "That's really all I've ever wanted. Just somebody to show me the way."

And so, after they were sure Sara under-

stood and that she was serious about her deci-
sion, Rebecca and Scott led her in prayer.
Together they helped her ask Jesus to forgive
her of her sins and to come into her heart as
the Lord of her life. Soon, before they even
knew it, all three were crying and hugging
one another. They knew it was just the beginning—that Sara would still have a lot to deal
with—but they also knew she was no longer
facing the battle on her own.

It was nearly sunrise when Aunt Myrna
agreed to drive Sara home. And after several
good-byes and a few more hugs, Rebecca
and Scott headed back into the house to get
some sleep.

"Can you believe it?" Rebecca said. "Everything worked out."

"It sure did," Scott replied. "Not the way
we thought it would, but better."

"That's the weird thing about God," Becka
said. "He never does things our way."

"Guess he just wants it done right." Scott
smirked.

"Guess so."

Becka was asleep before her head hit the
pillow. No dreams, no tossing and turning,
just sleep. Deep, peaceful sleep. Something
she had needed for days, and something she
finally enjoyed.

The next day flew by, and before long
Rebecca and Scott were packed up and riding
in the car back to the airport.

"Where're you going, Aunt Myrna?"
Becka asked as the car pulled onto the main
road and turned left instead of right. "This
is the way to Sorrento, not the airport."

"Oh, I know, honey, but I wanted to stop
by and show you something."

Minutes later they drove into Sorrento,
passed the library, and pulled up in front of
Pastor Barchett's church.

"What's going on?" Scott asked.

"Just hold on," Mom said. "You'll see."

They climbed out of the car and headed
up the steps to the door.

"Good," Aunt Myrna said, looking inside,
"we're just in time."

She opened the door wider, and they all
slipped into the church. There was only a
handful of others. But there, standing up
front in the baptistry—which was filled
with water—were Pastor Barchett and Sara
Thomas.

"And do you, uh . . ."

"Sara," she quietly reminded him.

"Yes, of course." He cleared his throat.
"And do you . . . Sara, fully understand what
you are about to do?"

Sara nodded, looking very solemn.

Rebecca and Scott watched in silent anticipation.

"Then—" the old man folded her arms in front of her—"I baptize thee in the name of the Father, and of Jesus Christ the Son, and of the Holy Spirit."

He lowered Sara back into the water, then lifted her again. She came out of the water looking radiant, water and tears of joy streaming down her face.

Becka and Scott joined the others in applauding. But there was another sound. Big, booming laughter. Laughter that could only belong to . . .

Becka spun around. "Big Sweet! What are you doing here?"

Big Sweet laughed again. "Why do you say that, Rebecca? I only tried to help Sara. I never wanted her to have such trouble."

Becka nodded. "You're right. I know that now."

He pulled his two daughters closer and continued. "My father, he taught me voodoo so I could protect myself and my family from bad spirits and curses. Sometimes it works—" he shrugged—"sometimes it doesn't. But this Jesus, this Son of *Bon Dieu*, the God of gods. There is much power in him. I will come by this church now and again to see what I see. What do you think about that?"

"I think that's great," Rebecca said.

"Me, too," Scott agreed.

"I just have one question." It was Aunt Myrna. "What about my goat?"

"I am sorry, Miss Myrna. It wandered onto my place and joined the others. I did not know it was yours. I will give you one of mine. I will give you two."

Outside, the good-byes were brief. "Come on," Mom fretted, "the plane won't wait."

"Did you hear the news?" Sara asked. "John Noey came out of his coma last night. And they think Ronnie Fitzgerald will be OK, too."

"That's great," Rebecca said.

"Looks like you got your first prayer answered," Scott said to Sara.

She beamed. "And your aunt has hired me to help her out a couple days a week."

"Well . . ." Aunt Myrna cleared her throat, a little embarrassed. "I can use a good worker like you around the house. Besides, I could stand a little company now that all my family is going."

"Oh, Aunt Myrna . . ."

There was another round of hugs and more than a couple of tears as everyone congratulated Sara and said final good-byes.

Then, just before Becka entered the car, Sara whispered something in her ear. Something Becka would remember for as long as she lived: "Thank you for showing me the real power," she whispered as she gave her a final hug. "And the real love."

~

Rebecca's heart leaped to her throat as she saw Ryan Riordan waiting for them at the baggage claim. He was everything she'd remembered: incredible black hair, warm eyes, and of course, that killer smile.

"Ryan!" Before she knew it, she had thrown her arms around him.

"I really missed you," he said, pulling her back to look at her and flashing his smile again.

"I missed you, too."

"What about me?" Scott broke in. "So who missed me?"

Ryan scratched his head. "Dunno, kid. That's a tough one. I'll let you know if I come up with someone."

Scott laughed in spite of himself. "I'll bet Cornelius did. That poor bird hasn't had anybody to squawk at or talk to for nearly a week."

The rest of the group laughed and agreed.

It was just like old times as the good-natured bantering and teasing began. But later that evening, when Ryan joined them at home and asked Becka to take a short walk with him, his mood had changed considerably.

"Beck, I've been waiting 'til we were alone to ask you something."

Rebecca caught her breath, hoping for some heartfelt words of romance. But when she saw the look in Ryan's deep blue eyes, she knew it was something else.

"I really worried about you while you were away. Is this going to be, like, a regular thing . . . running off to some faraway place whenever that Z guy contacts you?"

"Of course not!" She laughed in relief. "We haven't heard from Z for nearly a week. I'm sure this was just a one-time thing."

The tension left Ryan's face, and once again he broke into his killer smile. "That's good because I—"

"Hey, Beck!" Scotty was running out of the house.

Oh, great, Becka thought, not at all pleased with her brother's timing.

"There's a message from Z on the computer. It's about another place we need to go."

Her stomach tightened. "What?"

"Yeah, and here's what's really weird. He wants you to go without me."

"Without you?" Becka asked. "Why?

Where?" Scott paused, purely, she was sure, for dramatic effect. "Where?" she repeated impatiently.

He grinned and waggled his eyebrows. "Transylvania."

"Transylvania?" Rebecca was shocked. "Isn't that where all those stories take place . . . you know about . . . well, you know . . ."

"Vampires?" Scott said grinning.

"But vampires don't . . ." Her voice trailed off.

"Exist?" Scott asked.

Becka nodded numbly.

Scott shrugged. "According to Z, something over there has got some actress scared out of her wits. He wants you to check it out."

Rebecca turned to Ryan, unsure what to say.

But as always, he made it easy. "It's all right, Beck. . . . I understand."

"Oh, and something else," Scott said.

They both turned back to him.

"He sent a ticket for Ryan, too!"

Rebecca and Ryan stared at each other. Ryan raised his eyebrows.

"In the mood for a vacation?" Becka asked meekly.

Ryan tried to smile. "Sure, why not?"

But she was sure he was thinking the same thing she was . . . Transylvania? *Vampires* . . . ?

What was Z getting them into now?

AUTHOR'S NOTE

As we continue writing this series, I have two equal and opposing concerns. First, I don't want the reader to be too frightened of the devil. Compared to Jesus Christ, Satan is a wimp. The two aren't even in the same league. Although the supernatural evil in these books is based on a certain amount of fact, it's important to understand the awesome protection Jesus Christ offers to all those who have committed their lives to him.

This brings me to my second and somewhat opposing concern: Although the powers of darkness are nothing compared to the power of Jesus Christ and the authority he has given his followers, spiritual warfare is not something we casually stroll into. The situations in these novels are extreme to create suspense and drama. But if you should find yourself involved in something even vaguely similar, don't confront it alone. Find an older, more mature Christian (such as a parent, pastor, or youth leader) to talk to. Let them check the situation out to see what is happening, and ask them to help you deal with it.

Yes, we have the victory through Christ, but we should never send in inexperienced soldiers to fight the battle.

Bill